A Forbidden

Love Affair

STEVEN DELAUDER

Trafford rev. 03/15/2013

 www.trafford.com

North America & international
toll-free: 1 888 232 4444 (USA & Canada)
phone: 250 383 6864 ♦ fax: 812 355 4082

Dedication

I can't put into words how much this book means to me. It represents how my life is, how I want it to be, and how sometimes it can never be. This has been an amazing time that I'll never in my life forget and I have so many people to thank for it.

To Ariel:

You have been my number one fan since I started this. For someone as loving and thoughtful as you are to tell me that my writing is in your top five next to Stephen King and others is the single greatest thing anyone can ever say to me. The moment I put this book into reality you never once said that it was a bad idea or it was stupid. You kept on and you hung onto every word I wrote. For that, and for your friendship that I will never in my life take for granted I say thank you. And I thank God that he blessed me with you in my life.

To John:

Dude I never expected to think that you of all people would like this book in particular. You, like Ariel, have stuck by me since day one and I am eternally grateful for that. You are one of my closest friends and one of my best fans and you are always there to tell me that I did well and that you want more. Thank you, you helped make this book possible.

To Joseph and Tayshelle:

You guys as a pair have read chapter after chapter and it never really clicked inside of me. But I see now that you two have the same type of love as Lucas and Katie have. You know each other and you can feed off of the other person as you two carry on. Your support makes people believe in love, that love can happen to them. So thank you, you guys truly are awesome.

To Shawn and Jon:

Both of you remember when I wasn't at my best. You two keep me up when I don't want to be and when I want to be you always know how to make me laugh. Thank you both. I hold you both deep in my heart.

To Emily:

Thank you for keeping me alive. No one can understand how much I needed someone in my life as you do. You remind me of Nicole in this book because you have this great fire and passion and it inspires me to do better. Thank you.

To Mom and Dad:

You two have let me see the greatest things in life. I will never take your love for granted or your understanding. Mom, I love you with all of my heart and I owe every bit of this book and every part of my life to you because without your love and support none of this would be possible. Dad, you may have not been in my life until I was nine, but you taught me how to be a man. How to take responsibility. How to support myself. I will never forget what you have done for me nor will I forget the times we've spent together.

To Arianna:

You are my sister and without you I don't know if I would be the same person. You can't understand how much inspiration you give me every day to be a better person and a better uncle. I love everything you've done for me and you will always have a special part of my heart.

The chapters in this book, as well as the book itself are partially inspired by the television show One Tree Hill. So to the creator, Mark Schwahn, thank you.

Some of these chapters as you have read have been named after songs from various bands. I'm giving my thanks to Asking Alexandria, Rev Theory, Evanescence, Maroon 5, Creed, Fall Out Boy, Bullet For My Valentine, Serj Tankarin, Metallica, Train, Imogen Heap, Placebo, The Red Jumpsuit Apparatus, Andrew Lloyd Weber, KISS and Sum-41 for their songs.

And finally I want to thank the Lord Jesus Christ. Without Him I wouldn't be here, and I want to thank Him for the life I have been given.

Everybody, thank you. This journey is finally over.

Prelude

The cold night was useless against them. Even though the wind ripped through their bodies with brute force, the warmth of them holding each other and the love that exists between them was much too powerful for this cold city. His arms wrapped around her slim body gave him all the strength in the world, and all the warmth in his heart.

It was unfathomable how these two had met or why they were in love with each other but one thing remained clear as they held each other, life mattered. At least it did to them. I can't say it matters for anyone who reads this book, but if their story teaches you anything, let it be this.

"Tell me again." She asked of him.

"I love you." He told her.

The three little words that she had been waiting almost 4 months to hear finally came out in a slow but romantic way, and all she could do was smile as he pressed his lips to hers.

They didn't say anything else to each other for quite some time, because they didn't need too. They knew what the other one was thinking and if that doesn't tell you that they are meant to be, then I myself couldn't tell you.

Her name is Katie, and his name is Lucas.

And this is their story.

Katie

Katie Earnwright had what some people would call the best life. She was the top of her class as Eastgate High, captain of the cheerleading squad, and she was the girlfriend of the star quarterback, John Albright. She was raised by her father since the age of thirteen because her mother had passed on. The bond between mother and daughter is great, but in this particular case, it took some time for Katie to get over it. Her home life though, was as good as her high school life. Her life was 100% without a doubt perfect. But, as you know, these lives always take a turn for the worse, and for Katie, it all comes tumbling down. This is where our story starts.

It's a beautiful Monday morning here in Eastgate, and life couldn't be better if I tried to make it that way. Dad has already left; I'm starting to get worried about him. He's been tired more than usual, and I'm concerned he's overworking himself. Oh well, I'll talk to him if he gets home before 10 tonight, which I highly doubt.

I'm just about done with getting ready for school when my cell phone rings. It's John, ugh. This has been the usual routine for the past four weeks. He calls to see where I am and when I don't give him a definite answer, he yells at me for about fifteen minutes.

"Hello John." I said with a slight sigh.

"So, where are you?" He demanded.

"Where do you think? I'm at home, being pestered by my boyfriend because he's paranoid about me cheating on him."

"You didn't have to snap at me, you know."

"You don't need to call me every five minutes."

"I wouldn't have too if you just be honest with me."

"I am being honest with you! How many times do I have say that?"

"As many times as you want because we both know you're lying."

"Ugh, I'm not lying! I'm telling you the truth!"

"No, you're not. And I've had enough of it; find your own ride to school."

The phone went dead after that as I stood there with my mouth open. What did I do wrong this time? All I said was I was telling him the truth, and he hangs up on me? Fine, I'll just take the bus.

Things have changed with me and John, and it's starting to scare me. Don't get me wrong he's still the love of my life, but something's changed. He's never hit me so don't even start thinking it. Maybe it's because his parents just got divorced, although he says that's not the case. I wish things would go back to when I met John freshman year. He was so sweet and so understanding, and now he's this paranoid, stuck up quarterback. I guess the boy four years ago is just a memory, nothing more.

I'm on the bus when the driver makes his final stop and opens the doors to let on possibly the worst person in the world, Lucas Warren. People at school don't go near him, because he's the new kid, and the rumors are that he almost killed one guy back at his old school. He's what people would call a loner, and it's scary to even look at him. What's even worse, he's country, something us Eastgate northerner's can't stand.

He looks at me and rolls his eyes because the seat that I'm in is the only one left with a free seat. He sits down and says nothing, which helps me out in the long run because I don't want him to talk to me, ever. I close my eyes and think of John and let the memory take me away to a better place. The bus stops at the school drop off section and I go to first period, with Lucas Warren, the rebel behind me. This Monday is not going as planned.

Lucas

Lucas Warren was born in the rundown town of Clearance, Mississippi. He was born to a drunken family, where his mother ran off with every guy in town except her husband and that man in particular would turn to whiskey and vodka to heal his pain.

When Luke was four years old his father caught his wife in bed with his best friend. Three shotgun explosions later, Luke was an orphan. Seventeen foster homes later, he found himself in the north in Eastgate, Ohio. Unlike the girl in chapter one, his life is anything but perfect. But, the opposite effect will happen. His life is going to take a turn for the better.

I already hate today. I'm starting to get a little sick of this "going to school thing". Heaving myself out of bed, I couldn't get excited to get myself into the shower. I just didn't have it in me this morning; the effort was just not there. Whatever, I'll just spray on some AXE. Walking out of the bathroom, I noticed a note from my foster parents telling me I'll be home alone tonight. Fine, I've gotten used to it for five years.

I miss the south. It had this effect to it that made everything that much better. Here in Ohio it's not the same, because everyone here looks at me like I'm a freak. Just because I listen to "Free Bird" instead of "Bye, Bye, Bye" makes me a freak, whatever, it's their choice. Everything here is watered down and boring that it makes me want to tear my hair out.

I'm outside waiting for the bus when I see an old couple, Mr. and Mrs. Harrison. They have lived in Eastgate since the 1930's, and that's shocking how they could withstand being here in this city for over eighty years. Mr. Harrison is ninety—three, and his wife is ninety-two and they both look like they are going to kill over. I see the bus within sight; it's about five stops away so I figure it's going to take a while with the traffic.

The bus takes quicker than I had thought, so I get my bag ready and get ready for the strange and scared looks from everybody on the bus.

The reason I'm unpopular, well one of the reasons, is because last year at my old school I hit a guy in the back of the head with a skateboard. Word got around when I was arrested for attempted murder. The charges were dropped and I moved here three months into the school year. That Friday was my first day here, and it went exactly how I expected it to.

"Class, we have a new student today." Ms. Angel had said.

It's like I was child, like I was in the fifth grade. I had to stand there in front of the class and say my name, what my favorite hobbies are and all of that stuff. I was only in that school for about two hours and I was already called a. I ran into the guy who I knew I would have problems with, the "Football God" John Albright. It all started when I accidentally knocked his girlfriend's books over. What's her name again? Jessica?

I got on the bus, and as soon as I stepped foot inside the looks just came at me. I ignored it and tried to find my seat, but the only one I could find is next to this girl named Katie. She's pretty, but she probably thinks I'm nuts like everyone else. Oh well, doesn't affect me. The bus stops at the "beautiful" Eastgate High School and my excitement level has gone from zero to . . . . zero. The pure thought of school makes me sick.

Mondays suck.

Project

I'm late. My foster mom decided to let me sleep in and I didn't set my alarm last night. I've got detention for sure.

I didn't mind detention; it lets me be alone for a while, just a short while. It's hard to do that in a foster home.

I opened the door, avoiding Mr. Curtis' glare for being late and took my seat in the back of the class, away from everybody. I opened my book to make it look like I was doing something, and hardly listened to the teacher.

"As I was saying, midterms are just around the corner, and most of you, for example Mr. Warren, are failing this class." said Mr. Curtis. " I've told you in the beginning of the year you need Current History to graduate from Eastgate, and since most of you don't care about midterms, I'm assigning a midterm project, which ALL of you will participate in."

Ugh. Great, as if I needed anymore troubles. Now I've got to do a stupid project? Why in this Earth are teachers so evil? It makes no sense to me.

"Now I'm giving you three weeks to prepare for this project, and to make sure all of you do it, I will be assigning partners." said Mr. Curtis. "Yyvone and Jimmy, The Cold War. Henry and Paul, War in Korea. Katie and Lucas, the 1950's and beyond . . . ."

I stopped dead in my thoughts. Katie Earnwright? The cheerleader, the most popular girl in school? My project partner? I should have stayed home, if I had known that this was the day God punished me, I would have gladly stayed in bed.

She turned to look at me; her face was a mixture of emotions. She, like everyone else, thought me a psycho. Not only did it hurt me that everyone thought this, but I wanted them to know that I wasn't that bad. I was actually kind of good. But of course I'm stubborn, so instead I gave her a cold stare.

She winced, and turned around to stare out the window. She does this a lot. I think it's nice that she loves nature so much; sometimes I catch myself staring at her.

The class bell rang and I got up instantly, but Mr. Curtis had other plans.

"Lucas, Katie, come up here please."

Rolling my eyes, I walked up to him, standing alongside Katie, who again had a fearful expression on her face. I wasn't going to hurt her, I wouldn't dare do that to her. She was too much of a good person for me to hurt.

"Lucas, it's no secret that you and Katie don't like each other. I really don't care about that. What I care about is the fact that you do good work but you fail to meet the average grade in here." said Mr. Curtis. "I want you two to work on this assignment together, then go back to hating each other, but either way Lucas, you will need to get your grade up before finals, or you'll be held back a year."

I stormed out of his class, red in the face. I need a smoke; otherwise I'm going to rip my hair out. I turned around and I bumped into Katie, knocking her books over. Swearing under my breath, I bent down and helped her.

"Thanks," she said when I gave her the Pre-Cal book back, avoiding my look.

"You're welcome. So . . . I guess I'm going to need your number, so we can get this thing done."

She hastily scribbled down her seven digits, gave me the paper, and walked away quickly, looking back every few minutes to make sure I wouldn't kill her. I looked down at her number, smelling her perfume scent.

567-894-3024.

At least I got a girls number. Smiling, I tucked the number away, threw my bag over my shoulder, and made my way to my next class

Reality

I walked into my house slowly, checking to see if Dad was home. Of course he wasn't, probably off at another business meeting, which means leftovers from Sunday's big "family" dinner. I know Dad's been worried about me ever since Mom died, but a family dinner is supposed to be a mother, father, and child. But, he's my dad, so I guess he has to worry.

I went upstairs to my room, thankful that this Monday was finally at an end. Not only was John mad at me for not talking to him all day, *now* I have to do a report on the 1950's and beyond with Lucas Warren. Just the name gave me the creeps, and the way he stared at me when I looked back at him, there was nothing but pure hate in his eyes. I guess all hicks share a common hatred for us normal people. Whatever, if Mr. Free Bird wants to hate me then so be it, he's nothing more than an insect, nothing to me.

With disdain I called John, hoping to talk to him. He answered on the fourth ring.

"Hello?"

"John, it's me. Can we talk?"

"Sure, what about, the fact that my girlfriend wouldn't talk to me in school, but now that we're out she now wants to talk?"

"John, you're not being fair . . ."

"I'll tell you what's fair. Come over and get your things."

"Wh-what?"

"You heard me. I'm done with you and everything you bring. You're cheating, your lying, and your stupid attempts to try to talk. No, fuck that, we're done. Better yet, I don't want your shit near my house; you can come get it on the corner, where you belong. Just like your mother. I was stupid enough to be with your lying whore ass. Now I'm fixing it. Bye, don't even bother trying to talk to me ever again."

I stood frozen, like something had come out of nowhere and hit me directly in the chest, taking the wind out of me. John Albright just broke up with me, and called me a whore . . . I didn't know what to do or say. But the thunder and the rain came pouring down, and if he really left my stuff on the corner, it was sure to get ruined.

Driving down the road I started to bawl. The tears just kept pouring down my face, and it was hard to concentrate. I managed to find the corner and sure enough, there was my stuff, sitting in a damp cardboard box. I ran out and tried to lift the box up, but the rain had already messed up the box, and everything fell out the bottom. In a hurry I got everything up and I ran back to my car, crying and getting soaked. I slammed my car door and started it back up, and tried to make a U-turn, but all I did was manage to roll my car down the hill almost into the creek.

Swearing loudly I got out, and headed up to the main road. I looked around but there wasn't a house in sight. Then all of a sudden an old Ford pickup stopped and out of all the people I would've loved to not see, it was Lucas Warren hopping out. Running over to me, I quickly tensed up, ready to fight him if he tried anything.

"Katie? Is that you?"

Rolling my eyes I replied "Yeah."

"You okay? What happened?"

"I'm fine, just go back into your truck Lucas."

"Look Katie you're getting soaked let me take you home."

Well, I surely wasn't going to stand out in the rain and get sick was I? So I followed him into his truck, hopping in and shivering from the water all over me. He got in the driver's side, and started up the truck.

"What were you doing all the way out near Dear Creek, Katie?"

"What do you think? I walked? I rolled my car down the hill by accident."

"Do you need me to-?"

"I don't need you to do anything, Lucas. Just take me home."

I tried to keep myself from crying while I was in his car, I didn't want him to have the glory of seeing me hurt, but I guess I didn't do a good job because after ten minutes of silence he spoke.

"You okay?"

"Yeah," I said. "Just great."

He sighed and checked his backseat for something and came back up, handing me a towel.

"Is it your boyfriend?"

"I don't want to talk about it, especially with you."

"Why not?"

"Well, for one, I don't know you. For two, I don't really enjoy being in your company, and three I don't want my reputation ruined for being seen with you so you can just drop me off at the next corner, I'll walk the way back."

"Whatever you say rich girl."

He pulled over and I got out, slamming the door. I ran all the way home, opening the door and slamming it. I didn't bother seeing if Dad was home, I didn't care. I just wanted to take a shower and lie in bed and cry. I hated this day, I hated life. Everything didn't make sense. Why would John do this to me? Why would he say those things to me?

I curled up in bed, crying so hard I got a headache. I pulled the covers over my head and cried till I fell into a daze.

I dreamed about a bird that night, flying high over the others, free. I dreamed that this Monday never happened, and someone loved me. I couldn't make out his face, but he reached out for me, but before I could take his hand he disappeared, leaving me in darkness.

All over again.

favor

This rain is pouring down bad. I don't think I've seen rain this much in my life, and it was quite relaxing. I guess not everyone was enjoying it as much as me, as I watched Katie run towards her house and after making sure she could go inside, I restarted my old Ford and drove off, towards Deer Creek. If her car is damaged badly, I could get my foster dad, who runs Walter's Auto Shop on the main road, to maybe fix it up. I could use some of my money that I was saving for college, just as a favor to Katie. I wonder if she really meant what she said, about not liking me. To be quite honest there's sometimes where *I* don't even like me. But I put up with it just so there can be peace.

I pulled my truck over and got out where I picked her up, and walked down towards the creek, looking in any general direction. After a mile of walking, I saw it. It was an old fashioned Volkswagen Beetle, and it was in near perfect condition, with the only exception being the messed up back bumper and broken back window. I ran back up to the truck and drove towards it and hooked the tow to the bumper. I pulled it up and drove towards the auto shop, honking my horn when my foster father came out with an umbrella.

"What the hell happened here Luke?"

"This is Katie Earnwright's car. I was hoping we could fix it up. I found it in Deer Creek, open the garage before the rain ruins everything."

I pulled in and hopped out, unhooking the car and looked at it from the front. It seemed like there was nothing wrong, but on the passenger side it was scratched up pretty badly. The rear was busted up and the taillights were completely blown out. I sighed and went to the office.

"Dad, do you think we could fix this up tonight?"

"Tell you the truth Luke I don't even know why you care."

"What's that supposed to mean?"

He looked at me with a sullen look.

"Luke you know what I'm talking about. She's the daughter of one of the most powerful men in Eastgate, Ohio. Plus she's popular, and from what you've told me, she doesn't even know you exist."

"Yeah, but Dad, you didn't see her twenty minutes ago. She was hurt, emotionally. She was crying like there was no tomorrow. I don't think I've ever seen anyone like that."

He sighed and looked at the car.

"I can't do this job tonight, but if you stay overnight, get the parts and open up shop tomorrow before school, I'll get it done by noon."

"Thanks, Dad."

He left around eight, leaving me alone with everything. The first thing I should do, I thought, is call her house phone and see if she's home or not. I dialed the number but all I got was the machine. I didn't leave a message, but I did leave a callback number, just in case she wanted to see why the auto shop was calling her. I turned on the T.V., but as usual there was nothing on. So I turned on the radio and started to unload everything out from her backseat and trunk. I grabbed a notebook and a picture fell out. Picking it up I saw that it was her and her boyfriend, John. She was smiling but he wasn't. Weird.

I put everything on the table and called the shop down in the next county to see if they had the parts. They did, and said the shipment would be dropped off around eleven forty five in the morning, which was perfect timing for my foster dad to fix it. Ignoring the radio, which was blaring about another body they found in Toledo by the Toledo Butcher, I called my dad.

"Dad, the parts are coming in around noon."

"Perfect," he said. "Now make sure you close everything down before you turn in for the night okay? Night son."

"Night Dad."

As I laid in the back room, strumming my guitar and thinking about anything in general, I began to wonder. If Katie didn't like me, she wouldn't have allowed me to take her home. But then again she was pretty damn rude to me when she was in my truck, so I guess it's a 50/50. I put the guitar back and turned in for the night, tired as all hell.

My dream was weird. I dreamed I was a bird, flying high above every other bird, free from everything. I dreamed that somebody loved me, and that when I felt her touch my entire body was filled with warmth. But as I got closer to seeing her face, she vanished into the darkness, leaving me all alone.

Change of Heart

I woke with a jolt. My alarm clock was playing something on the radio, but I was way too tired to make it out. I got up, took a shower and tried to contemplate what had happened last night. The last thing I remember is getting my stuff from the corner near John's house.

John. I forgot he dumped me last night. I tried to remember anything after that, but I think I cried the memory away.

I opened my phone and called him, and he answered on the third ring.

"Hello?"

"Hey, John . . . can we talk?"

Then he said the one thing that I would never forget.

"Do I know you? Don't call this number again."

The sharp sound of him hanging up the phone made me jump. I threw the phone across the room and it hit my mirror, which then fell to my floor. I hugged my knees and started crying, and I guess it must've alarmed my dad, because he knocked on the door.

"Katie, Katie are you okay?"

Wiping my tears away I responded "Yeah Dad, I'm fine. Can I get a ride to school?"

"What's wrong with your car?"

My car! I forgot it rolled into Deer Creek! "Nothing, I just want to be with you for a few."

"Sure, I'll drop you off."

I breathed a sigh of relief, and hurried downstairs. I hopped in my dad's Jaguar and waited for him to come out. I'm shaking, from head to toe, wondering what people are going to say. I'm dreading this day already.

I get dropped off and I head directly to my first hour, Pre-Cal. Mr. Gregg is a cool teacher, he lets me sleep when I have to. But today I need comfort, and he's not the type of teacher for that. My friends are all talking behind my back, and it hurts me to know that they probably have been doing this all along. I have no one to turn to.

Around noon I couldn't take the snickering anymore. I ran to my locker, crying heavily when someone came up next to me.

Great as if my day couldn't get any worse, Lucas Warren.

"Hey Katie. Are you feeling better?"

"I'm fine Lucas, just go away."

"Look if you need someone to talk to-"

"I said leave me alone!"

I slammed my locker and started to walk away when he said something that startled me.

"Your car's in the lot!"

I stopped dead in my tracks. I turned to look at him, and I was startled when he threw me my keys. I looked at them with surprise and when I looked back up he was walking away, rather fast. I felt shocked and bad for snapping at him, but I couldn't just stand there. I grabbed my keys and headed out to the lot and sure enough, there it was. My car, fully fixed and better than before. He put everything I had in my backseat in a brand new bow, and even fixed the seats. I got in and started the car, and it ran perfectly. I couldn't believe this!

Why did Lucas Warren do something nice for *me?* I sure as hell wasn't nice to him.

I got out and headed back in, looking for him. He was standing at his locker, messing with things. I walked up to him uneasy.

"Why did you fix my car?"

He didn't look at me. "I couldn't just leave it in the creek. Don't bother paying me; I took out my own money."

I was open mouthed. "Thanks, Lucas."

He was glaring into the locker. "Don't mention it."

I turned to go away when he spoke again.

"Not everyone is talking about you, you know."

I turned back to face him and he spoke again.

"I'm really sorry about you and John. I mean that."

All I could do was nod.

He closed the locker and looked at me with understanding eyes.

"Curtis wants our report in by the Monday after next. I guess I'll be calling you soon. See you later Katie."

He turned, walked towards the corner and walked out of sight. I was frozen with a mixture of confusion and thoughtlessness. I realized that I had to leave because of the final bell, and I went back out to my car.

I sat there for about thirty minutes thinking. Maybe I was wrong about Lucas Warren, the boy from the south. I started my car and headed for home, still thinking about the boy from Clearance, Mississippi.

New Friends, Same Enemies

I got home around four-thirty. I looked at the note from my foster mom, Christina. I love her, she's the perfect mom. I can talk to her about anything. She let me know that pizza's in the fridge and Walter needs me in the shop. Great, work. I love working on cars, it's what I've wanted to do since I was six.

I had dinner and started up the old Chevy Walter said I could use. While driving, I got a glimpse of John Albright, not even a day out if his relationship and he's already holding hands with Jessica Smith. Rolling my eyes I pulled into the main road and parked the car into the lot and entered the shop through the side entrance.

"Dad?"

"In here Luke!"

I entered the office, looking at my dad, and then turning my head towards Mr. Earnwright, Katie's father.

Everyone in Eastgate knew who Bob Earnwright was. He was the most powerful man in this town, next to the mayor, who turned to Bob for his banking account. Mr. Earnwright was an investment banker, and everyone who was with him is living on Western Ave.

"Hi Dad, Mr. Earnwright."

"Please," he said, extending his hand. "Call me Bob."

I shook his hand and looked at Walter.

"So what's going on?"

"I was just telling Bob about what happened last night."

I looked at Bob. He smiled "I can't thank you enough for doing what you did. You're quite a young man."

I smiled. "It was no problem. Really. So, Dad, what am I doing in the shop?"

"Just the usual. Mr. Walters muffler gave out again, I think it's time we got him a new one."

I was just fixing up someone's bumper when Walter called for me.

"Luke! You got a visitor!"

I looked up and there was Katie, standing in the garage doorway. I tried to keep myself from smiling, and walked over to her, wiping oil on my t-shirt.

"Hey." I said.

"I'm sorry for disturbing you, but I just wanted you to know I really appreciate what you did. And I think it's in all fairness that I pay you something."

"Oh, it's fine. I paid for everything, and I'm not accepting anything from you."

"Are you sure? It's a lot of money."

"I think it'll be okay. Are you feeling any better?"

She tensed up, and squinted. "I've been better. But I'll be okay. He's already dating again; I guess I wasn't good enough."

I frowned and looked at her stunning blue eyes, and tried to find the words to say. "If you need anyone to talk to, I'm here."

"I'll be fine. But if you want to start on our project tomorrow, I get off of work at five. Stop by then."

She turned and walked away, leaving me staring at her until I realized she was gone. I walked back into the shop and went back to work when Walter came up to me.

"What was that about?"

"She just wanted to say thank you. No big deal."

I looked away, trying to concentrate on my work but the thought of Katie kept clouding my mind. I managed to finish my work and got back into my car, closing my eyes and breathing deeply. I need to clear my mind. I got an important study session with Katie tomorrow, and I can't be so pent up with thoughts about her.

When I got home I fed my dog Leo and went up to my room, turning on my radio and played my favorite CD, Nevermind from Nirvana. I sat on my bed, trying to focus on my Trig homework, but I couldn't do it so I put my books away and laid down on my bed, looking up at my fan.

Tomorrow at this time I would be at Katie Earnwright's house, doing a report.

I only hope I can concentrate.

New Light

I'm going to scream if I can't find anything to wear. My partner Lucas is coming over tonight for our project and I can't figure out what to wear. The only thing I have is my skinny jeans and my really nice blouse, but that's for when I went out with somebody, like John. I sure as hell don't want Lucas thinking I'm into him.

Although, to tell you the truth I kind of am. I don't know what it is about him but he's surrounded by mystery and he never shows it. He's so . . . . strange it's quite appealing. The way he walks, and the way he says things . . . . it's like he's from a different planet. He's kind and sweet.

But on the other hand he's a hick, a lowdown scumbag who hates everything about the north, including northern girls. Ugh, I threw on an old shirt and some faded jeans, he doesn't deserve me looking my best, I mean after all this must be what country girls wear right? Like they just walked out of the gutter.

The doorbell rings and I'm too late to answer it, my dad beat me to it.

"Hey Luke." Said my dad. "What brings you here?"

"Hey Mr. Earnwright, I'm here to see Katie. We're uh . . . partners for a class assignment."

"Oh? Katie never told me, but then again she's a seventeen year old girl, she never tells me anything. Hold on one second, I'll get her."

I ran back to my room and pretended like I was reading a book when he knocked.

"Katie?"

"Yeah, Dad?"

"Lucas Warren is here, says you guys are partners for an assignment?"

"Yeah . . . I'll be right down."

His footsteps faded and I sighed. Here we go, time for me to slowly explain to him what history means. I got downstairs and saw him standing in the doorway, he was holding his backpack over his shoulder and was wearing a faded tee and some ripped up jeans. For a split second my heart stopped, but I cleared my throat and walked down the hallway.

"Hey, Katie." he said.

"Hi. Look I don't like this anymore then you do, so let's just get this over with, okay?"

"Whatever you say, rich girl."

Rolling my eyes I led him into the dining room and sat down.

"Do you want a drink?"

"No, I'm fine. I just want to get this done so I can pass."

"Fine, so what do you want to do?"

"Well I was thinking and since we're doing the 1950's and beyond, maybe we could make a timeline of all the events, starting with the 1952 Congress meeting to discuss the relationship between the Soviet Union and the United States, the 1955 race riot in Clearance, Mississippi and then we could-"

"Wait, slow down. How do you know all this stuff?"

"I read . . . . a lot. I like to read."

I nodded, listening to him talk and taking down notes. This kid was smarter then he looked. I kept looking into his grey eyes and smiling a few times, and then glared into my notebook to stop myself. He finally stopped talking and we got to work, making notes, reading up facts and drawing up a timeline. I felt this was solid A work, he really wanted to pass this class.

We got done around eight forty five and after he had put all of his stuff away, I wanted to ask him something.

"Is it true, what everyone says?"

He looked confused. "About what?"

"About why you came here."

He stopped and looked down. I could tell that this was a touchy subject, and I didn't want to upset him.

"I'm not as bad as you make me out to be. I made a few mistakes, who hasn't? I just wish people would take the time to get to know me, know my situation. Like my friend Nicole."

"Nicole Lewis?" Nicole was the resident bookworm of Eastgate. She was always the odd one out when it came to high school.

"Yeah. She's a good friend . . . . my only friend. Anyway, she's the only one who knows the truth."

I paused. "And what's the truth?"

"That I never tried to kill anyone. That the only reason I'm here is because of what happened to my parents."

"What happened?"

"My mother was the Jessica Smith of Clearance, and one night she was with my father's best friend. He lost all control and killed both of them, and then he killed himself. I was only four. So, I was placed in the system. Seventeen foster homes later here I am, a senior at Eastgate High School, about to graduate and leave this state forever."

I couldn't even express the shock that was just put through me. He sat there, looking down at the table and glaring, and I was in total shock. It's like he shed new light on my view of him and now there's not a doubt in my mind that he was dealt an unlucky card.

"I'm sorry, Luke. I really mean that, I am. I don't know why no one has ever wondered."

"Yeah well, I should get going; I've still got a lot to do. I'll see you around Katie."

He turned and walked out the door, and hearing the distinct sound of an engine, I knew he was gone. I walked upstairs and passed my dad's office when he called me.

"Katie!"

"Yeah Dad?

"How was it? Did you guys get a lot of work done?"

"Yeah, it was good."

"You know, that boy has been put through a lot of hell. It's nice to know my daughter is kind and gentle to him."

"Yeah . . . night Dad."

"Night sweetheart."

I flopped on my bed and closed my eyes, sure that tonight I would dream of Lucas Warren.

Crossroads

My phone ringing in the middle of the night was the one thing that scared me. It always sits on my chest and every so often I get calls. This time though I made the exception as I saw Nicole's face on the caller ID.

Nicole was the first person I met when I came to Eastgate. I could tell by the way she saw me she knew I wasn't as bad as they made me out to be. She was kind and that same day we became best friends. We talk for hours at a time on the phone, and since we were so good to each other, we ignored every rumor about us dating. There was a time where I did in fact like her in that way, but we talked it over and we decided it was best to remain friends.

I answered on the third ring.

"Hey Nicks." That was my nickname for her.

"Guten Tag sleepyhead. What time is it over there?"

I checked my clock. "Almost four in the morning. When are you getting back?"

"We're at the airport now, about ready to board. See you in about nine hours."

I smiled. "Great, I'll pick you up. Bye."

She hung up and I went back to sleep, waiting for my alarm to go off.

I woke up around seven thirty, alive and ready for Nicole to come home. But first I had to go over to the shop and do a few things, and after that I had to go and see my probation officer. He's a stern man but he's very understanding. I ran back home and started up my car, pulling out of the drive and headed up to the airport. It's about a three hour drive, because we don't really have an airport, we use the Toledo Airport.

Things have gotten bad up here in Toledo. There's this serial killer on the loose, named the Toledo Butcher, and he's got at least thirteen plus dead bodies under his belt. There are police stops every five blocks and they go through everything you have. I checked out okay and I took the highway to the airport. I sat on my hood, waiting for the phone to ring so I can find her and get her home. We haven't seen each other in nine weeks. I've missed her so much, and today we're going to have the best damn day we can hope for. It's going to be the only day I see her, because tomorrow I'm going over to Katie's again for our project.

Things have clearly changed for me since I've been here. I've gone from one friend, to one friend and a sometimes friend in Katie. She smiles when I pass her in the halls, and we have some good small talks in between classes. It's like she's accepted me for who I am, and not following the rumors anymore. I smiled to myself, almost forgetting that my phone was buzzing.

"Hello?"

"Luke, where are you? I'm at the front desk."

"Okay, I'll be there in a minute."

I drove around to the main building and walked through the front doors, searching for her when all of a sudden I was being attacked by a five foot four blur of blonde hair.

"Hey, Luke!" she said.

"Hey, Nicole. How was your flight?"

She let me go. "Oh you know bad movies and even worse airplane food."

"Uh huh and how was Germany?"

"It was amazing! I got you at least six things from six different cities. Come on, let's go."

"Wait, where are your parents?"

"They're staying behind for a few more days. They'll be back next week."

On the drive back she was chattering about everything she did, and everywhere she went. She was blabbering away while we were at the police checks, and even on the way home. I dropped her off because she had to do a few things, so I told her to meet me at the shop. I drove over and I was working when Katie knocked on the wall.

"Hey, Luke."

I wiped my hands off on my jeans, cleaning the oil.

"Hey, Katie. I thought we were working tomorrow?"

"I know, but I wanted to see if you were in."

"Well, I'm here. What can I help you with?"

"My car is making a changing noise in the engine, and I don't know a thing about cars so . . ."

"Bring it in." I moved my Chevy.

She backed in and I opened the hood, meeting a whole bunch of black smoke hitting me in the face. I coughed and blew the smoke away.

"So, can you fix it?"

I smiled. "Of course I can."

"Ummm, hey Luke."

I turned around to see Nicole standing in the doorway.

"Oh hey, Nicks." But she wasn't listening to me; instead she was glaring over in Katie's direction.

"Okay, so I'll call you later Katie, and I'll get you an estimate."

"Okay, see you tomorrow Luke." She smiled and left, not looking at Nicole, as if she wasn't even there.

"What was Miss High and Mighty doing here?"

I grimaced. "Her car is damaged. Plus she's my project partner."

"Sucks to be you. Hope John doesn't kill you."

"Actually, they broke up. Or rather he dumped her."

She laughed. "Serves her right."

I sighed and went back to working on the engine, not wanting to say anything to Nicole on her first day back.

But the sad part is, I was falling for the person my best friend hates most on this Earth.

Great.

Attractions

As I walked down my street, I began to think about what had just happened between me and Lucas. He had this look on his face . . . . like he was conflicted with something, with someone. I had never seen this side of him before, I always saw the dark twisted and hateful side of him. It turns out that he was human, he was kind. He never took anything for granted and he was always considerate. It makes me smile, it makes me feel warm.

I never quite understood what makes people hate other people. When my mom was alive she always told me that no matter what happens in this world, as long as you can see the inner beauty in somebody, they are worth loving. So I always tried to see the good in people but with Lucas, I only saw this hateful person who only cared about himself. I don't know why I didn't try to see the other side of him and I don't know why I let John control that part of me. I guess people learn from their mistakes.

I turned my corner and what I saw shocked me to my very core. John was sitting on my porch, holding a bottle of what would appear to be whiskey. He looked up at me, and smiled trying to stand up. He was off his ass drunk and from what it looked like he'd been drinking for a few hours. I knew that when he drank he was in a violent mood, but he'd never hit me. I knew John, he wasn't this person. But that didn't stop me from taking a step back when he advanced on me.

"Hey." He said. "You look good."

I looked down, and fumbled with my keys. Now would be a great time for Dad to get home.

"You need to go."

He smirked. "What's that supposed to mean?"

"Nothing, you just need to go."

"Come on baby, you know you don't mean that."

"Yes I do. Go."

"You need to listen to me-"

"I think you need to listen to her."

I whipped my head around and there was Lucas, standing by his car. John laughed once and looked at me.

"What's this punk doing here?"

When I couldn't answer he looked at him again, advancing towards him. I reached for my phone to call the police, but Lucas was one step ahead of me.

"Look I'm not looking for trouble, just do what she said. Go."

"You going to make me?" He pushed Lucas, and tensed up. I didn't know what was going to happen but all I knew was I was going to call the police, but my finger had barley pressed nine before Lucas threw his fist into John's jaw. He fell, and got up what seemed to be automatically.

But what happened next was amazing. John didn't do a thing, all he did was hold his jaw and pick up his bottle. He turned and looked at me.

"I don't need this, and I don't need you. Bitch." He walked away and I looked at Lucas.

"You okay?" He asked me.

"Yeah, let's get you some ice. Come inside."

He followed me in, holding his hand, which was already swelling. I had him sit, and I went into the kitchen to get him come ice. I wrapped it up in a washcloth, and tied it. Walking back in I was still amazed at what happened. I was scared of what John could do but I was . . . kind of turned on by what Lucas did. I mean I was terrified, but I liked how Lucas stood up for me. John never did, all he did was laugh at what people said to me.

I handed him the bag and sat down, staring at him. I guess I was staring pretty hard because he looked at me.

"What? Look I'm sorry I punched him, he just-"

"Oh, no, it's not that. Trust me; I know how he is when he's drunk."

"Well he's a jackass.'

I looked down. "He wasn't so bad. He was just really hard to manage."

"You shouldn't have to manage someone. Sorry."

"It's okay." I smiled.

"Well I guess I should go. I got to fix your car, it won't fix itself."

I nodded, and walked him out. He turned and looked at me.

"You shouldn't have to manage him. Because he doesn't deserve you."

I was stunned, even after he got in his car and drove off I was still standing there, smiling. I closed the door behind me and walked up to my room, and flopped down on my bed. I closed my eyes and smiled. Lucas Warren was in dreams for the fourth night in a row.

Sweet Dreams

I checked my phone for the time. It was getting late, and I only had five blocks to go from Katie's house. I still had the ice pack she made for me because my hand was in serious pain. I only wish I got a few more shots in that jackass's face before my hand started to swell. I guess I'm not as tough as I thought.

I turned down Lancaster and made my way towards my house when I heard a weird noise. I turned around, but it was nothing but a dog. What can I say, I'm paranoid. I just punched out the star football player, the most popular guy at Eastgate. I was almost sure that he was plotting something right now with him and his friends. They're only like this because football is starting soon.

The way Eastgate works is basketball is the fall/winter sport, since we've been known for our basketball more. Eastgate has twenty-three sports state championships. Basketball owns seventeen state titles, track and field owns five, and football has one. That was twenty years ago, and ever since then our twelve game season has managed four wins per year. Ever since John got to the school though, our record has been somewhat decent. Last year they went 8-4, and lost in a playoff wild card game, the first since the state title victory. He's a good quarterback; he just needs the wide outs to get the job done.

I walked onto my porch, and sitting on the porch was a package for me. I picked it up with my good hand and walked up to my room and put the box on my bed. I went back downstairs to eat, and do my homework. Katie and I's project was due next week and we already had it done. We worked well together; we had the will to be good with each other. Sure there were times where we didn't see eye to eye, but we talked it over and we were fine. I caught myself in a daze, and I went back upstairs. I opened the box and first picked up the note:

"Don't wear it unless you're sure you want this."

Confused, I put the note down and picked the second thing out of the box. It was an Eastgate Lion football jersey. I put it on my bed. I looked at the note again; it had no signature, no nothing. I can't believe someone knew I played football as a kid, and I was good. I looked over at my trophies, and I smiled. I remember playing alongside my friends from Georgia, at my last foster home. I won Best Wide Out and Most Valuable Player that year. I looked back at the jersey, and picked it up. In a daze, I tried it on and looked in the mirror and my reflection looked back at me, wearing the number eighty-eight. I smiled and picked up my phone, and called Nicole. She was sleeping, judging by her growling voice.

"What, Luke?" she growled.

"I'm going to be an Eastgate Lion, Nicks."

"Are you on drugs?"

"What's that supposed to mean?"

"John is the quarterback. After you punched him, who knows what he's going to do to you."

"How did you know-?"

"It's all over Facebook. You're in some serious business."

"What did he say?"

"Just that you ambushed him as he was trying to get Katie back. What were you doing over there anyways?"

"I just . . . . I needed to see Katie about our project."

"Well, you're not going to enjoy the next few days at school."

"Well I'm still going to play. I just wanted you to know."

"K, night."

I hung up and closed my eyes, sighing. I am so screwed.

I was going to play football, and the captain was my enemy.

Ironic, huh?

Heaven's on Fire

I woke up late on Saturday for two reasons: one, I really didn't want to get up, and two I had another dream about Lucas last night. That's five nights in a row that I've had a dream about this boy. I sat up slowly, groaning. I didn't want to get out of this bed, but I've got to get down to the auto shop to get my car. I need my car; I'm actually kind of sick of getting a ride from Dad. It's just been awkward being around him lately, there seems to be something off about him. I always ask him how work is but he just shrugs it off like I never asked him anything. He's already gone, so I made my own breakfast and as I was sitting there, I caught a glimpse of the local newspaper sports section:

"Eastgate Lions season three weeks away!"
"The Eastgate Lions will open their regular season play three weeks from this Friday at eight p.m., against hated rival Blackfoot. The Lions went 8-5 last year, losing in the wild card round to LaSale in double overtime, 34-31. What will this season hold as John Albright leads his team out onto the field for the last season? Three weeks from this Friday, eight p.m."

I groaned again. I totally blanked out on this season starting; I was so preoccupied by John and Lucas. I went back upstairs to change and headed from my house to Main Street. During my walk I noticed people were already getting prepared for the season, they were sure that our school was going to win it all behind John. What they don't understand is that we need more than just John; we need someone else to actually catch the ball. We won't win more than nine games this year, that's a fact.

I turned down Main, and saw that the light was on in the garage. I smiled and as I was walking towards it, I remembered my dream about Lucas. We were standing in a meadow, holding hands. We didn't say anything, we didn't do anything but look at each other and as soon as I tried to lean in to kiss those thin lips of his, he vanished, leaving me with nothing but silence.

I knocked and Lucas answered. "Hey Katie, your here for your car?"

"Yeah, just need to get it and-"

But I stopped, because I overheard the radio.

"And breaking news coming from the office of Lions head coach Bill Jones, the Lions have added a new player to their roster, effective the first game. Jones has stated that the new player is Lucas Warren, at wide out! Who knows what this addition will do to the already dominate offense of Eastgate. That's all for now, from Eastgate Lions radio, KBG-106.7"

I looked back at Lucas, who was standing there, with an odd expression on his face. I looked over and saw the football schedule posted up on the wall and shook my head.

"Are you insane, Luke? Do you know what John is going to do once he hears this?"

"Look I had nothing to do with it." He said. "I got back from your place and the package was sitting on my porch."

"So you're going to play football for Eastgate?"

"I'm thinking about it. What's the big deal Katie?"

"The big deal is that you're going to get yourself hurt! And the sad part is it won't be from the opposite team!"

He sighed and went behind the counter and handed me the keys to my car, and wrote down the bill for the repair. I looked into his eyes and there was hurt in them, but I didn't know why. All I could think about was how much this is going to suck if Lucas decides to play. I don't think that this is going to be fun for anybody, but there's nothing I can do.

I pulled up into my driveway and got out. Dad was waiting for me on the porch, and from what I could tell; it wasn't a good day at work.

"Hey, Dad." I said.

"Hey, Kat."

"What's going on? Is everything okay?"

"Hmm? Oh, yeah. Everything's fine. Just needed some fresh air."

"Okay, I'll be in my room if you need me."

I went upstairs and closed my door. I took a quick shower and got back into bed, but all I could think about was Lucas . . . . in an Eastgate football jersey. With his scruffy blonde hair, his grey eyes, and his tall, muscular body. Just thinking about it . . . turns me on. I smiled and went to sleep, almost sure that this dream was going to be hot.

I saw him at the end of the hallway, me wearing my cheerleader's outfit, him in this football outfit. I jumped up into his arms, pulling at the back of his hair as our lips met in a fury of excitement. He had his palm on the back of my head, forcing my mouth onto his, moaning just a little bit. I pulled more at his hair, as his hands found the zipper to my skirt . . . .

I woke up covered in sweat, and looked around my room. I flopped my head back on my pillow and breathed heavily. I didn't want to wake up. I wanted to stay with him, together, locked mouth to mouth. It was clear what was happening to me.

I was falling in love with Lucas Warren.

Practice

I was not at all looking forward to after school. It's the first practice and I'm nervous as all hell, and if you ask me it's not because I'm going to be playing football. It's because I was not looking forward to practicing with John, or his friends. I had already expressed my concerns with the coach, but all he told me was it's nothing to worry about.

"He's like this with everyone. You just got to ignore it and focus on work ethic. We want to go to state; we're going to need all the help we can get."

Ugh, something tells me that everything he said was complete and utter bull. I went to my locker after the bell to get what I needed, my pads, my helmet and everything. I sighed and pushed the door open to the locker room, and the first one to greet me was none other than our team captain, and the guy who I punched in the jaw just two nights ago.

"Well well. Look who's here boys, good old southern garbage." He said.

"Look, I don't want any-"

"Any what? Trouble? Gee that's too bad, because trouble found you." And just like that I felt hands grabbing me from all angles.

During my useless attempt to get myself free from what they were about to do, I got a good look at some of these guys. The only thing I noticed about them is that they were all seniors, every single player. These guys had to deal with John for four years, and they are all like him, the sad thing is they will never see that.

They threw me into the shower, which was by that time blistering hot, and they stood in front of the only exit point out so I had no choice but to sit there and take it. I glared right at John, every part of my body wanted to pound his face into the ground. But instead I just glared, and waited for someone to speak.

"You know, the easiest way for this all to be over is to just quit. Before something worse happens, because trust me, it will get worse. Just quit man, you don't have what it takes."

As they all left, I looked down, realizing that John may in fact be right on this case. I don't have what it takes to be a player on this team, because the person who runs it won't give me a chance to be a player. To them I'm nothing, nothing but scum off their cleats. So what I did was change into my equipment, and, dreading the practice even before it starts, opened the door to the field, where the group was already kneeling down to hear a talk from the coach.

"First practice and your already late. Take a knee; I'll deal with you later."

I nodded and took a knee, looking over at John. He was smirking, and shaking his head. This must be fun for him, for him and all his buddies. Wait until we get a few snaps in, I thought. I'll show them why I belong on this team. I'm just as good as them. I know this, and I'm going to prove it to them.

"Alright guys. First off, I want you to welcome Lucas to the team. Although he may be late and will run suicides till he pukes after practice for being late, he's still a hell of a player. And I want all of you to make sure he's comfortable on this team. God knows he deserves it."

I wasn't expecting any clapping, but I did get a few pats on the shoulder from the kid to my left. He wasn't one of the guys from the locker room, so I knew he wasn't messing with me. I smiled and looked back at the coach.

"Second thing. I want you all to take a good look at this field. Because this is the last year that you will play football as an Eastgate Lion. The last time you will wear blue and silver. The last time you will get a chance to go to state before you graduate. Because this entire team is full of seniors, I want all of you to go out with a huge bang. And that bang is the state championship. Now last year we won eight games, and we lost four regular season, and one playoff game. In the first round guys, the first round. To LaSale, a team who went 5-7 and barley won their division. John threw four picks in that game, two went back for a touchdown. That will not happen this year, and you know why? Because we will win ten games this year, and we will go to state. Or we will all go out trying. Because this is also my last year."

I looked around at the guys, and they were all muttering and had looks of shock. All but one and you all know who that is. John was still smiling, the biggest look of cockiness in him. This guy was so full of hot air it was really pathetic, so pathetic that it was funny. But I shook it off and looked back at the coach. I knew he still had a lot more to say.

"So guys, let me ask you. Do you want to go out in the first round, or do you want to prove to the state of Ohio that you are still worth something?"

The yell was so loud that it took me by surprise, but I took part, because there was a fire that was inside me that was amazing. I wanted to win that state title, I wanted it so bad.

"Alright then, let's go to work!"

I stood up and put my helmet on, looking to my left and there she was. Katie was with the other cheerleaders, and that fire was burning more. I smiled, and as soon as I knew she was watching, I ran to the huddle. John was already there, kneeling down and looking at me head on.

"Okay, hick. You think your good, prove it. Eighty-eight slant. Eighty-eight slant, on one on one, break."

I was running a slant? I guess they really do want me dead, but I shrugged it off and took my spot on the field. The guy across from me was smirking, just like John. I knew this was a setup, I saw the middle linebacker shift to his right, towards me. By the way John was setting up; I knew as soon as I looked at him, he'd gun the ball at me. So I planted my feet and prepared for it.

"Twenty-two, black cross, ready! Hike!"

I bolted forward, and made my route. I saw for a split second that the safeties were advancing towards me, leaving all other wide outs open. I looked at John, and saw a blur of brown coming my way. I jumped and caught the ball, landing on the ground, but instead of getting ready for the hit, I spun to my right, faking the middle linebacker out and leaving me with open field. I took my advantage, and ran like a bat out of hell towards the end zone. I juked a safety and dived over another one into the colored turf.

I stood up and looked back at everyone; everyone's face was in total shock. John was livid, Katie was smiling, and the coach was open mouthed.

I smiled and headed back to the huddle, knowing we were going to win that state title.

Bliss

We rolled around on the bed, wrapped in each other's arms. I felt his hand move up my leg, but then he slid it down, like he was afraid of something, afraid of going further with me. I released myself from his lips and whispered in his ear.

"It's okay," I said. "I want you."

He looked at me, with his warm grey eyes tearing in my soul, and in an instant, he kissed me again. His lips were careful as he went down my trembling body. I closed my eyes tight as I felt his hand reach up for my shirt button. I helped him the best I could, but he was in charge. I never had to lift a finger as he unbuttoned my shirt and climbed back up to me so I could kiss his amazing lips once more. I couldn't believe that this was happening but I didn't care. There was nothing that could tear me from him. Not a damn thing.

His hands grew impatient, so I laughed and reached down to undo my jeans, but he wouldn't have any of it. His hands were in charge, and they did the rest. Soon enough my jeans were lying useless on the floor with his shirt and mine. I clawed his back hard and he responded with a soft bite to my neck, but even that drove me insane with passion. I moaned softly into his ear, and begged him to keep going; I couldn't take this teasing much more.

I unbuckled his belt and felt his jeans slide off, and now we were totally in our natural suits. I whispered in his ear to not be afraid, and he slowly adjusted himself between my legs . . . .

My alarm clock starting blaring in my ear, and I sat upright in a flash. I was covered in sweat and was breathing heavily so I went to the bathroom to splash water in my face. I looked at myself in the mirror, and tried to get a grip on myself.

That dream last night felt really real, I wanted it to be real so much. I sat down on my bathroom floor and cried for a good twenty minutes. Even in my dreams I couldn't have him, I couldn't have Lucas. I sat up to take shower, and after getting out and getting ready for school, I wanted to ask him out so much, but I was afraid of what he'd say. I didn't want him to become John.

I went downstairs and looked over to see if Dad was home, but of course he wasn't. I sighed and got in my car, and headed for school. I could barely concentrate in Contemporary History because I was so amazed by him. I decided I was going to at least talk to him, I mean after all he's on the team, and our first game is this Friday, so I want to wish him luck.

The bell rang and I jumped up, and waited for him to get ahead of me. I saw him glance my way and smile, and every bit of me melted on spot. I took a deep breath and followed him, waiting for my chance to get him alone.

"Lucas!" I called.

He looked back, confused, but smiled when he realized it was me.

"Hey Katie, what's up?"

"Oh, nothing. Just wanted to see how you're doing, what with the game being this Friday."

"I'm uhhhhh . . . . trying to convince myself that I didn't make a mistake. Also, I'm trying not to throw up."

I laughed, and judging by his face, I was acting weird, so I calmed down and smiled.

"Walk me to lunch." I said.

He smiled and nodded, walking alongside me.

We talked about random things, everything from the game to school. I tried not to make myself seem to desperate, but I couldn't help myself. I decided I was going to ask him.

"Hey, Luke. I was wondering . . . . what are you doing after the game?"

He looked confused. "Not too much, I guess. Just probably going to go home. Why?"

"I was just wondering if you maybe wanted to hang out. Just . . . as friends?"

He smiled and showed his amazing, white teeth and I tried not to melt right there.

"Sure Katie, I'd love to." After that he hugged me and headed towards the music hallway and left me to go to lunch, and although I was calm on the outside, I was screaming like hell on the inside.

I just asked out Lucas Warren, the outsider from Mississippi, on a date . . . sort of.

I know I should worry, but all I could do was smile.

fourth and Sixteen

"**W**ell I don't know what to tell you folks. The Eastgate Lions are down 21-16 in the first game. John Albright has failed to see that new comer Lucas Warren has managed to get open on almost every single pass play, but he just has not tried to get to him. I don't know what he's doing out there he's 3 for 15 tonight, and those 3 completions have been for at least three yards. It looks like the Lions will start at the bottom of the barrel at a 0-1 record. Only time will tell, this is the last chance for the Lions, fourth and sixteen from their own thirty eight yard line."

I was out of breath, not from getting receptions. I was out of breath from yelling for the ball so much, from yelling at the coach because I got so wide open down the field, and John refuses to pass it. We're down by six, with three seconds left. Fourth down, sixteen yards to go. We clearly need to pass the ball, and I clearly need to get open. I know John doesn't want to lose, but I also know he knows about me and Katie hanging out after the game. I went to the huddle to await the call.

"Alright guys, we got one shot. One shot to get this in, so hick!" He said, and I looked at him. "Don't screw this up."

I nodded and went to my slot to get ready. I scanned the field and saw that the safeties blitz after every five yards of passing. So I knew they were going to blitz on this one, so I planted my feet. I was running a cutback, so I knew that it wasn't going to be a scoring play. I waited, and knew what I had to do. I looked over at John.

"Blue twenty two! Blue twenty two! HIKE!"

I didn't even bother with my route, all I did was fake the corner to the left, and then spun around two safeties and was all alone going down the field. John noticed that and took the bait, and as he flung the ball my way, I looked up and saw that it was about to land in my arms. I caught it and only had ten yards to go, and as the roar of the crowd erupted, I ran the ball into the end zone and turned around to meet about six of my teammates jumping on top of me. I had just won my first high school football game.

I ran to the sideline and caught a glimpse of Katie. She was jumping up and down in her cute cheerleader outfit, smiling only at me. I smiled back and went to the coach who hugged me and took the ball from me. I laughed and got in line to shake hands with the other team. I saw their faces, all of them hated me. I felt good, because I was hated for a real reason.

I walked into the locker room, getting high fives from everybody, but John was standing by my locker. Arms folded, and a glare on his face. I sighed and prepared for it.

"Great route. Could've sworn I said cutback, but I guess running a full straight against three defenders is okay."

"I got open didn't I?"

"Yeah barley. We'll see next week when we're up against Trenton. Good luck."

I shrugged and got dressed; I was getting ready to go hang out with Katie.

I saw her waiting by my car, looking down in thought, so I smiled and advanced on her. I wasn't quite sure what we would do, but as long as I was with her, I was fine.

Before I could say a word, Nicole was attacking me from behind. I knew it was her because her punch felt like a fly had tapped me on the shoulder. I turned around anyways, so I could tell her the good news that I was going to hang out with Katie, but judging by the look in her eyes, I knew that it wasn't the time for that.

"Nicks, what's wrong?"

"You're hanging out with *her?!?!?!?!?*"

"Yeah, what's so bad about her?"

"Oh I don't know everything? Luke, don't you see that she's just using you to heal her heart? She's still in love with that asshole, and she's using you to make it all better, but as soon as it is . . . you will be nothing to her."

I was stunned and hurt at the same time. I just could not believe that Nicole, my best friend, would say that about someone. This sweet, innocent little bookworm was now full of hate and anger towards someone, and that someone was the girl that I loved. So I glared and turned around.

"Luke! Did you not hear me or do I have to spell it out for you?"

"Look Nicole, you don't know anything about her."

"Oh, and you do?"

"That's not the point. At least I'm trying to make an effort, your just choosing to hate her, as if she didn't even exist!"

"You didn't know me last year; you don't know what she's capable of."

"Well then I guess I'm going to find out, won't I?"

I turned around again and walked up to Katie, who smiled and hugged me, wishing me congratulations on the win. I thanked her and opened her door for her and walked over to the driver's side. I looked at Nicole again, shook my head and got in. I knew I was going to have fun with Katie tonight; I didn't need Nicole's permission to have fun.

At least Katie said congratulations to me.

Voices

found Lucas' car out in the parking lot. I had just got done getting out of my outfit, put it in my locker and got dressed quickly. I had on my favorite pair of jeans and a low cut shirt, call me a slut but tonight was my night with Lucas and I wanted to look nice. I was sitting on his hood looking quite sexy when the weirdest thing happened. It was like this voice in my head started talking to me.

"You know that was the outfit you wore in your dream."

I was stunned, but quickly squashed that feeling once I saw Lucas. He was walking towards me when Nicole hit him, but I guess it was friendly, so I stood and waited until he was done. I looked at my outfit and realized that that voice in my head was right. This was the outfit I wore in my dream a few nights ago. I looked up at Lucas and saw that his outfit was the same from the dream. I gasped and looked around, wondering if anyone noticed me. I caught a glimpse of John walking out, surrounded by tons of people for his heroic game saving touchdown pass. I rolled my eyes and looked away; it's Lucas who should be the hero. He's the one who was wide open, not John. But then again John was the quarterback, so I guess it's him that gets the glory.

I saw Luke heading my way so I stood up and hugged him, smiling on both the inside and out. I looked over at Nicole, who met my look with pure hatred and contempt. I figured she had the right, seeing as me and her have a pretty bad history. I looked away and looked up at Luke.

"Congrats on the catch, Luke."

He smiled and my heart did a backflip.

"Thank you. Let me get that for you." He opened my door for me, and I smiled at him.

"Thanks." I got in. I looked in the mirror one more time and smiled. I was ready to make my move.

Luke got in and smiled, starting the car. "So," he said. "Where to?"

I smiled. "I know the place."

He laughed and pulled out of the parking lot, and got on Main Road. We talked about everything, from the game to what John said about Trenton. I assured him that Trenton was the worst team on the west side of Ohio; they have not won a game for three years. I looked at him, he was so . . . . . sexy. He had his sandy blonde hair everywhere from his helmet, and his grey eyes were full of happiness instead of hatred. It was a better look on him, with the turf still in his hair. I rubbed my legs together, trying to control myself next to him. I told him to turn down Hawk Lane, towards the cliffs.

We pulled over at the edge of the cliff, overlooking our small little town. He was looking at everything, awe in his face. I had never seen him so in love with life. I was always aware that he had a loud hatred for Eastgate, but I could tell that was all changing. Tonight I was going to give him another reason to love this town, me. I wanted so much to straddle him and take off his clothes, but I knew I had to take it slow.

"So, Luke. I noticed you have been smiling a little more lately."

He laughed and looked down, playing with the steering wheel.

"Yeah, I guess I have been. I guess some of the credit goes to you."

I smiled wide and opened my mouth but that voice came back.

"For God's sakes, girl kiss him!"

I looked out the window, and looked around. I shook my head and looked at Luke, who had a look of confusion on his face.

"Sorry, thought I heard something."

We started talking and didn't realize that it was three in the morning. He decided to run me home, and along the way the voice was yelling at me, using every word to tell me that I was a chicken. We pulled onto Western, and pulled up in front of my house. I invited him in and we went up to my room. He sat on my bed and I sat in front of him.

"So, have you ever?" I asked.

"Ever what?"

"Come on, Luke. We're in my room. Have you ever had sex?"

He laughed and sat up.

"No. I haven't."

"DO IT, NOW!" shouted the voice in my head. "DO IT!"

I sat up, and looked at him.

"Want me to teach you?"

He stared at me and leaned in a little. I leaned in as well, and our lips met. The slow movement of his upper lip on mine sent waves of pleasure throughout my body. I grabbed the back of his head and increased the pressure of our kissing.

I laid him down and got on top of him, not letting our kiss cancel. I couldn't let this end, not at all.

We rolled around on the bed, wrapped in each other's arms. I felt his hand move up my leg, but then he slid it down, like he was afraid of something, afraid of going further with me. I released myself from his lips and whispered in his ear.

"It's okay," I said. "I want you."

He looked at me, with his warm grey eyes tearing in my soul, and in an instant, he kissed me again. His lips were careful as he went down my trembling body. I closed my eyes tight as I felt his hand reach up for my shirt button. I helped him the best I could, but he was in charge. I never had to lift a finger as he unbuttoned my shirt and climbed back up to me so I could kiss his amazing lips once more. I couldn't believe that this was happening but I didn't care. There was nothing that could tear me from him. Not a damn thing.

His hands grew impatient, so I laughed and reached down to undo my jeans, but he wouldn't have any of it. His hands were in charge, and they did the rest. Soon enough my jeans were lying useless on the floor with his shirt and mine. I clawed his back hard and he responded with a soft bite to my neck, but even that drove me insane with passion. I moaned softly into his ear, and begged him to keep going; I couldn't take this teasing much more.

I unbuckled his belt and felt his jeans slide off, and now we were totally in our natural suits. I whispered in his ear to not be afraid, and he slowly adjusted himself between my legs.

Satisfaction

The birds chirping and the warm sunshine from the window was not the thing that awoke me on this morning. The thing that awoke me was the goddess on top of me, smiling in all her beauty. Nothing was covering her up, but she didn't care. I smiled and held out my arms. Her smile was too much for me in the morning, her smile and everything about her. I grabbed a hold of her waist and smiled back up at her.

"Good morning, sexy." She said.

I laughed. "Good morning beautiful."

Blushing, she replied. "Sleep well?"

"Nope. I was too busy with last night to sleep."

"Oh? Which part were you busy with?"

I sat up and held her to me. "A little bit of this."

I kissed her softly, feeling her heartbeat against mine. It was like we were in tune with each other, and let me tell you, I loved every minute of it. I pulled away and kissed her neck hard, moving my hands down her body. I was met with her hands clawing at my chest and I was not sure if it was because she likes it or she wanted me off. I pulled my lips off of her neck to look up at her.

"Why'd you stop?" She asked me.

I smiled at her and rolled over so that I could be on top, but the sound of a car pulling into the driveway stopped me dead in my tracks. I looked down at her and she pushed me off. Swearing, she threw her shirt and shorts on fast and pushed me into her bathroom with my clothes. I got dressed and looked at myself in the mirror. I smiled, both on the inside and out. *I had sex with Katie.*

I tried to figure out just how it had happened, but about five minutes into trying, I realized I didn't care. All I could think about was her, and her body and her lips and just about everything that we did last night. I lifted up on my shirt and looked at the claw marks on my chest and laughed silently. My first time with a girl and I got marked. How lovely.

I listened to see if she was coming up and sure enough, she bolted into the bathroom and closed the door.

"Hey there." I said.

"Shhh! Listen, you have to stay here for about ten minutes okay? My dad is home and if he sees you, he'll kill me."

"Okay, but uh, Katie?"

She turned around to look at me.

"Are we . . . ?"

"Dating? Only if you'll call me your girlfriend."

My heart did about fifteen backflips and landed on its feet. I was dating Katie Earnwright, the rich girl on Western Ave. I had sex with her, now I'm dating her. In just five weeks I went from hating her to being head over heels in love with her, and this was just the beginning of it. I was jumping for joy inside my mind, but on the outside all I could do was smile.

She left and I waited ten minutes and when she gave him the clear, I ran downstairs and met her at the front door.

"So . . . I'll call you later?" I asked.

"Mmmmm maybe. Depends on what I'm wearing." She smirked and kissed me.

I kissed back, not wanting to let go, not wanting to leave. But I had to, and after about a good ten minutes of making out at her door, I walked outside and got in my car. Starting it, I made a U-turn and pulled onto Main Road, in the direction of my house. Along the way I saw that the people were still cheering last night's victory, and as I smiled at them I thought about everything I had been through in my life, and how it was going to feel like once we won the state championship. I smiled and loved every moment of it, every singular second of last night was replaying in my head.

I saw that Nicole was waiting on my porch when I pulled in and as I got out and smiled at her, her face was a totally different expression. Walking up, I saw that her hair was a mess and her makeup was smeared.

"Nicks, what's wrong?"

"I have something to tell you, Lucas."

"Okay," I said and sat down next to her. "What's going on?"

"I did something really stupid last night."

I looked at her dead in the face. Nicole, doing something stupid? Now I knew something terrible had happened.

"Lucas, I slept with John last night."

My Own Prison

"**A**lright ladies, that's enough practice! Hit the showers!" I screamed.

We had just got done with our afternoon routine, and I was sure we were going to kick ass next game against Trenton. Lucas will too, the hot stud he is. It was hard for me to concentrate on my practice with him in my mind. It was like having this really great dream, and you want to relive it every night. Except mine was real, real and amazing. Of course, we couldn't let people know about us because it would destroy us both. John would wage World War III on us, and there would be no end to what he would have to say. So no matter which way you looked at it, we were stuck.

I walked over to grab my bag when a shadow overcame me. I turned around and there was John, standing over me wearing this strange smirk over his face. I rolled my eyes and started to walk away, but him and his damn cockiness followed me. So I turned around and looked at him dead in the eyes with every bit of coldness I could muster.

"What do you want, John? I'm busy."

"Easy tiger, I just wanted to see how you were doing."

"How I'm doing? I'm heartbroken, I'm stressed, and I'm late . . . . for work."

"Okay, fine. Don't let me keep you waiting! Sorry I ever asked!"

He walked away, and I made my way to the locker room when he called out for me.

"By the way, you're not the only one who fucked over Nicole. Just thought you should know."

I rolled my eyes again and walked into the locker room. I threw my bag in my locker and walked into the shower. After I got out, I got dressed for work and left the school. On the way I started to think about Luke, and about how amazing last night was. Thinking about him and what he could do made me shudder and breathe heavily. So I decided to stop and let my mind wander about work.

I pulled into the parking lot of Patterson's Diner and walked inside. I've worked here for about six or seven months and I have to say, the pay isn't that bad. The customers are mainly old folks, except for Fridays this time of year. I'll let you be the judge on that one. I walked into the back and got my apron. I had just enough time to go to the bathroom, because I'm feeling sick. I found the stall and released the mouthful of vomit that had just come up on me. I choked a bit and flushed the toilet, crying a little. This was a terrible feeling I was having, and I couldn't explain it. But I didn't have time to think about it because my boss came into the bathroom.

"Katie?" she called out.

"Yes, Mrs. Jennings?"

"You okay, dear?"

"I'm . . . fine. I just got a little bit of morning sickness."

"Okay well maybe you should take the day off. We wouldn't want the customers to eat puke with their hot cakes."

"Are you sure? I could always-"

"No, dear. We can manage. Go home."

I sighed and got up opening the door and, avoiding Mrs. Jennings look, I grabbed my bag and headed out the door. Slamming my car door, I started it up and pulled out so fast I almost hit someone driving down Main. I tried my best to focus on the road, and even while that was happening I was thinking about what happened.

It couldn't be it just couldn't be. I was on birth control, I knew that much already. The awkward doctor appointment five years ago with Dad . . . ugh. In fact it was five years ago . . . *yesterday.* The birth control only lasts five years, and my five years was up YESTERDAY! I put the brakes on and made a sharp U-turn, heading for Mike's General Store.

I was there in five minutes, and after I pulled in I flew out of the car and ran inside. Slowing myself to a walk I went to the parenting section and scanned the items until I found what I was looking for. I picked up the pregnancy test and went to the counter.

Mike Hardaway looked at the test, then at me then back to the test. I looked out the door and waited until he gave me the price. I wish he didn't stare so much.

"Two eighty eight."

I gave him a five and didn't even bother with the change. I picked up the box and ran to my car. I pulled out and made my way towards Western, hoping to God what was going through my mind wasn't true. I pulled into the drive, and bolted to my room. I went to my bathroom and followed the directions on the box. It said it needed about ninety seconds to work so I set it down on the sink and paced back and forth.

I looked at myself in the mirror and looked at my stomach. I stared at it until I felt sick again, so I emptied out my stomach and looked at myself again. I couldn't be . . . pregnant. Could I? Everything points towards yes, but maybe the ring has effects that last longer than the time frame. Or I could've gotten the date wrong, just off by a little bit. I'm only hoping that for once my mind was wrong.

A minute passed, and my hand trembled as I picked up the strip. I looked at it, then at the box and gave out a sharp breath.

Second Thoughts

I laughed. For two reasons, one was because I knew what Nicole had just told me was a lie. The other reason was because somewhere in the back of my mind I knew that if this thing with her and John were true, I knew that I was going to have a fun time pounding John's face into the dirt. I looked over at Nicole and her face told me that what she said was true. I felt like I was just kicked in the gut, so I stood up with a reaction that made her jump a little bit.

"I'm sorry, you did what?" I said.

"I slept with John last night."

"John? John Albright? You slept with the biggest jackass in Eastgate? You're aware of that right?"

"Well you slept with Eastgate's biggest skank!"

"This has NOTHING to do with Katie! And so what if I did?"

"Lucas that's not fair, you weren't here a year ago, you don't know the real her."

"Like I said, this has nothing to do with Katie. Why did you sleep with him?!?!?"

"I don't know. I was standing in the place where you left me and he walked over and offered me a ride home. It was about to rain and I didn't want to walk."

"Okay, so he gives you a ride home. And what, your thank you is taking off your clothes and giving him a ride of his own?"

"Will you let me finish? We got to my house, and I was going to just say goodnight and leave, but he started to talk to me and I talked back and next thing you know . . . . we had sex."

"So what, you guys dating now?"

"I don't know . . . maybe. Are you and Katie?"

"I don't know . . . maybe."

She shook her head and looked at me.

"Luke, don't trust her! She's not the great person you think she is!"

"Neither is he."

She started to say something, but decided against it and looked at the sun.

"When did it all get so messed up, Luke? Why can't we just go back to the way we used to be?"

I looked at her, and told her the truth.

"You left for nine weeks."

She nodded, tearing up. I held her and kissed the top of her head.

"Everything is going to be okay, Nicks. We'll be okay."

My phone vibrated in my pocket, and I picked it up, seeing it was Katie.

"Hello?" I said.

"Luke?"

"Yeah, it's me. What's up?"

"This may sound . . . totally shocking, but I think . . . . Luke I think I'm pregnant."

fear

I heard the dial tone on Lucas' cell, and only one thing came to my mind. He freaked, and now I'm alone. I paced my bathroom floor feeling sick and afraid that Lucas was going to leave me. I couldn't believe it, I was honest with him. I made sure of that, I told him everything. I'm thinking so hard it's giving a headache, and the headache is driving me to tears.

I sat on my toilet and looked at my stomach. Could it be possible that I had a living thing inside of me right now? I just didn't want to believe it right now. Nothing made sense anymore, Luke won't want this baby. John would claim it as his, but I don't want that. I didn't know what I was going to do, I didn't know if I was able to face my father. No one at school would accept me, my cheerleading scholarship would vanish and college wouldn't even be an option.

I got up and looked at my reflection. I didn't know how bad this was or how bad it could get, nor did I want to. I got a rush of sickness and rushed to my toilet. I coughed and wiped my mouth, flushing the toilet in the process. I put my head between my knees and cried a little. I felt like total crap both on the inside and on the outside. But what could I do?

I was stuck no matter what; no matter how hard I tried I was stuck.

I was pregnant.

I started crying even more, more than when John dumped me. More than when my mom died more than . . . more than when Dad told me he was sick. I couldn't believe I was going to be alone again. It just hit me like a ton of bricks falling on top of my face, like a piano falling on me or a nuclear bomb going off right above me. I looked at the strip again and it read the same thing: blue. I closed my eyes and just let the wave of emotion take over me.

We were just starting out, Lucas and I. And now we have a baby together, and all because we didn't have protection.

We should have waited, but I was so damn enticed by him I didn't care about the repercussions. Well look where it got me, look where it got us. We're probably over even before we started. I didn't want to lose him, but if he doesn't want this child what choice do I have?

I heard a loud knock on the door so I got up and slowly walked to the front door downstairs, thinking to myself whoever it was, they were going to have a bad time. I was not in the mood to deal with anything today.

But when I opened the door, I looked at the visitor. He was tall, and had sandy blonde hair. His grey eyes cut through me like glass and his stare was mysterious.

He wasn't leaving me, he was seeing me.

Lucas Warren was standing at my front door.

Repercussions

I about jammed Katie's doorbell with how many times I pressed it. I wasn't totally caught up with myself, the hours kind of blurred from the time I left Nicole's. My body was one place and my mind was in another. From the time I got Katie's call to now was twenty minutes; I left as soon as I got her news.

My girlfriend was pregnant.

That word keeps flashing in my mind like a damn sign. I didn't know whether or not to be happy or upset. It was only last night we were together, so she shouldn't be pregnant. Not now at least.

The door opened and there she was still in her morning clothes. I stood there for a minute not sure if I should hold her or if I should ask what happened. She smiled and I knew I had to hold her, to feel her touch against my body was all I ever yearned for. I closed my eyes and just let her cry into my shoulder for a minute because it was all I could do.

I broke us apart and wiped away her tears. I smiled at her and she led me up to her room where we had our night of amazing love. I closed her door and took a good look at her. She was not in the best of moods, that became clear the first time I saw her. I sighed and sat next to her, letting her drain herself of every tear and sob.

I kissed her head and spoke softly, "Shhhhh. it's okay, it's okay."

Her tear streaked face looked up at me, "How can you say that?"

"Because I know in my heart that if indeed you are pregnant, I won't leave you."

"You can't just say that. You can't just be okay with the fact that I'm pregnant."

"But I am. We don't even know if it's true."

"But it is I know it is."

"Well we will just have to wait on it."

She nodded, and I knew the subject was changed. For now. But I stood up and held her softly, kissing her ever so gently. I couldn't bear her pain any longer, for it hurt me to see her so unsure and lost. I tensed up and held her a little harder. I didn't want to leave her side. I never wanted anything more than her happiness. Even if it meant being a father to her child that I possibly had.

We broke apart and I kissed her again. Then another, and another. I whispered in her ear that I would protect her and we kissed and fell to the bed. It was clear to me at that moment the feeling I had was more than infatuation.

I was fully, in depth and undeniably in love with Katie Earnwright.

Harder to Breathe

It was Friday. Game night. We were at home against Trenton but it was hard to concentrate on cheerleading or football for that matter. I still hadn't told anybody about my condition or that Lucas and I were dating. It was so hard to consider that there was still another world outside us that still mattered. Not only to me but to him as well. If, on the off chance this pregnancy is a false alarm I want him to stay, but on the good chance that I am carrying his child I don't want him to feel obligated to stay. It's his choice if he wants to be a free spirit, I won't stop him.

Walking into the locker room, I caught stares from everybody because they had all seen me leave with Lucas last week. It was weird to think that it was only last week that Lucas and I made love. I say made love because it wasn't, nor is still about sex. Maybe at first because I was still pent up over John but now I really feel something for this guy. The way he looks at me, like I'm the only girl in the world. Like I'm the only one he'd want to see if something went wrong, His smile and his charm made me feel like gravity has no effect on my body. There is nowhere I'd rather be then in his arms, in his comfort. I can be myself around him and in that freedom I find myself saying things I really feel. He made me happier then I could ever imagine.

My daydreaming was hindering my focus, as all of a sudden I found myself staring into space when I was supposed to make an announcement to my squad.

"Girls, I got some bad news. Heather broke her leg while visiting her grandmother this weekend, so we're one short tonight. So Jen and Amber will have to double it. Okay?"

Their faces were a mixed bunch but they knew what I say goes. After all, I'm head cheerleader. Then Ms. Davis, our coach, knocked on the door.

"Katie, someone's here to see you."

I nodded and took a drink of my water. The girls' random chatter died when I turned around because there he was. My boyfriend, Lucas Warren. He was already in his uniform and he was looking pretty nervous due to the staring,

"Luke, what's up?"

"Nothing, I just wanted to inform the squad that the party tonight is at John's mothers. Not his father's. Also, good luck out there Katie."

He winked at me and I about melted again. His effect on me is out of this world, but it was unfair that I won't get him tonight. He is such a tease!

I zipped up my skirt and looked at my reflection, most notably at my stomach. I smiled and looked away, but had to look back. I knew that whatever was going to come next would be for the better. I anticipated a storm though, because I knew that this relationship would be tested on all levels. Parents, best friends, ex's, everybody will be trying to break us apart. But I knew in my heart that Lucas Warren would be mine forever, because I know in my heart I was going to have a family with him. That feeling is too strong to be incorrect.

Me and my squad arranged ourselves and waited for the call.

"And now, before the pride of your Eastgate Lions, please welcome our lionesses! Ladies and gentlemen, led by squad leader Katie Earnwright and Coach Davis, your nine time National Cheerleading champions, the Eastgate Lionesses!"

I smiled, because the rush of football is one great thing.

Being in love is another.

Wins to Losses

"Okay guys, huddle up!"

John's orders couldn't be clearer. He was irritable for everything tonight. He was nine for thirty two, with only 185 passing yards, no touchdowns. I had only three receptions for about twenty-two yards. For some reason that I did not know, I couldn't get anything going tonight, I guess Trenton got pretty good.

"Alright men, we're down by three, and its third and four. I want to run slant twenty four. Slant twenty four. Break."

I was blocking, so I didn't have to worry about anything. All I had to do was make sure Mark, our running back, made it for four yards. Then we were in the clear to tie the game.

"Ready! Blue eighteen, blue eighteen! HIKE!"

I charged forward, and did my best. I got my hands under his collar and pushed off. I thought I had done a good job, but I heard a whistle and a yellow flag was thrown my way. I took a step back for a minute. I never had a hold on him for more than three seconds.

"Holding eighty-eight, Eastgate! Ten yards!"

I walked up to the ref, seething with rage.

"You're kidding right? I held him for a second and pushed off!"

"Son, I saw holding. It's done. Go back to your sideline."

I shook my head and ran back to the line, making my anger apparent. I took off my helmet and prepared to get torn apart by the coach.

"Son, you just cost us the game! It's third and fourteen, we've got no timeouts, and there is twenty seconds left on the clock!"

"Coach, I wasn't holding!"

"It doesn't matter! We got called for it!"

I put my head down and just gave up. I knew I wasn't going to get through to him. I just got chewed out and put my helmet back on. Running to the huddle, I had the play in my head. I looked at John and the guys.

"Eighty-eight streak, John."

"You're serious?"

"Coach said eighty-eight streaks."

"Well we're not running it. You just cost us the game. I'm not putting the ball in your hands. Eighty-five spike eighty-five spikes."

I rolled my eyes and got in my place. I wanted this to be over. This is the third time he's changed the play to avoid me getting the ball.

"Blue seven, blue seven. HIKE!"

I ran, cut through the defenders and was wide open on the right side of field. I turned around and saw he was looking dead at me, but just did not throw it. I waved and saw him throw it, but not to me. The ball went over Jack's head and into the arms of the Trenton defender.

The crowd quickly died as did I. I was in the end zone, alone. No one was near me. Yet he didn't pass the ball because he wanted to be the hero. I shook my head and went to the locker room. I looked up at our scoreboard and it hit me in the chest.

Trenton-24, Eastgate-21.

I got out of my uniform and threw it in the basket. John came in with a scowl on his face and singled me out automatically.

"Hey! Where were you on the streak!?!?!?"

"ME? Where were you when I said eighty-eight streaks! You changed the play! AND, I was wide open!"

"Whatever! You cost us the game! Some player you are!"

I clenched my fists and turned away. Hit him, lose everything. Walk away, win next week.

I picked up my bag and walked outside. I saw Nicole walking up, and stopped because I have not talked to her in a while.

"Hey, Luke."

"Hey."

"Sorry about the loss."

"Yeah, me too."

She turned and saw Katie leaning up against my car and sighed.

"Well, I'll let you get back to your new life."

I shook my head and walked past her, and up to Katie. I knew I was fine, as long as I was with her. She was my everything now, just like Nicole said. I have a brand new life now.

And it was a damn good one if you ask me.

Get Busy Living or Get Busy Dying

I was in such a terrible mood. Not only did John cost us the game, from what I heard he tried to put the blame on Lucas. The nerve of him! I want nothing more than to slap him upside his big fat egotistical head. I hated him. I hated him for the fact that not only did he dump me like a bag of hammers; his arrogance grew about ten times larger since then. I threw my uniform in my bag and stalked out of the locker room so fast I didn't hear my friend Stacy calling me.

"Katie!" She called speed walking down the hall.

"Oh, hey Stacy. What's up?"

"You are going to the party?"

"I wouldn't even if I was in a good mood."

"Well I heard Lucas will be there." She said with a slight smile.

"What does that have anything to do wi-"

"Come on Katie, I saw you looking at him tonight. What's going on?"

"We slept together. Last week, and we've been kind of dating."

"Wait, what? You and Lucas Warren?"

I nodded, smiling.

"Katie you can't be serious."

"What do you mean?"

"Katie, come on. He's different. You know this goes against everything you know right?"

"Stacy, I'm dating the guy it's not like a religious law that says I can't."

"There might as well be. Katie, he hates being here. You know as well as I do, as soon as graduation passes he's gone.

Why waste your time on someone who isn't willing to stay for you?"

I shook my head and backed up.

"Look, I've got to go Stacy. I'll call you later."

I turned and walked out of the side entrance. I didn't even stop to glare at Nicole; I just didn't want to do anything but see Luke. I'm sure I can make his bad feelings go away tonight. I walked over to his car and leaned against it, waiting for him. But I got a visit from the one person I didn't want to see.

"What the hell are you doing leaning against this loser's car?" John demanded.

I stood up, and glared at him so bad he actually took a few steps back.

"I don't see why it's any of your business. What do you want, John?"

"Look I don't want any trouble, but I don't want your loser boyfriend near my place you got that?"

"He's not my boyfriend, he's my friend. And I wasn't even planning on stepping foot on your disease infested property. So now that you came to say what you said, you can leave."

He glared and stalked off to see his dad. His father, who recently divorced his mom and she left town, was a banker who didn't hesitate to berate his son at the first possible moment. I used to feel sorry for John, now I'm wishing I taped the time he actually made John cry.

Luke walked up and smiled at me. I smiled back and couldn't wait to get him all to myself tonight. This time we'd be using protection if it came down to it.

We started talking as he drove us to his place, and I was ready for him. I was ready for us.

I was ready for forever.

Turn for The Worse

I could tell that something was making Katie upset. She was silent the whole car ride home plus she just wasn't her usual self. I didn't know if it was because we lost or it was something else that she wasn't telling me. I looked over at her, she was sitting in the seat with her hands across her chest and her glare was on the road. She looked over at me and smiled, reaching her hand out and held my free one. I smiled back and kissed her hand while still paying attention to the road. I knew something was still upsetting her but she'll tell me eventually.

I turned onto her road and stopped right in front of her house. I kissed her slightly and breathed sharply. It was killing me that I couldn't have her tonight, and she was going out of her way to tease me. I didn't like it one little bit.

"Okay, well I guess I'll see you later Luke."

"You don't have to go now, do you?"

"Mmmmm I think I should, because if I don't", she slid her tank top down, "I might do something I'll regret later."

I sighed and kissed her neck softly feeling her tremble a little.

"You better stop, or my jeans will just magically appear in your backseat in the morning."

"Keep talking like that and they will. Good night, Katie."

I kissed her again and opened her door for her. She smiled and got out and as I watched her walk to her door I couldn't help but notice that she hasn't brought up the baby in a couple days. Maybe that's what's bothering her.

I knew she was excited about having my baby, but I'm not so sure she was actually pregnant. I think her body is just messing with her, and I don't know how to tell her.

I pulled out of her driveway and set off for my house. As I began my way I began to think about how she could be pregnant. It didn't seem possible but she could be. There's a one in a million cases each year but it happens. But the chances of it being mine were totally nil. There was no way it was mine, but I'm not saying I don't want it to be. To be honest I would love to be the father of her child. But there is just no possible way it's mine.

I stopped at a red light and used the time to gather myself. I needed to find some way to tell her that it wasn't mine. I know her reaction won't be lovely but she has to know that the baby, if she is pregnant, can't be mine. I know it sounds bad but I have to be honest with her.

The light turned green and I turned left onto Main. But as that happened I saw a blur of white lights and everything went dark. I felt the car roll over and heard the sounds of tires screeching and the sound of an engine fading away, as if the car was leaving. I was pinned down by the wheel and I could feel myself getting tired. The pain suddenly drifted away.

What Goes Up, Must Come Down

I saw Luke turn away and walked into my house. I didn't know if Dad was home or not, but I saw that there was a letter for me on the table. It was from the hospital, where I had checked myself out due to my pregnancy. I ripped it open and scanned over it before I actually sat down to read it.

To a Miss Katie Earnwright,

We regret to inform you that your blood tests came back negative. This is not common in your particular situation, and we strongly advise another appointment be set up as soon as possible. Our office hours are from eight in the morning until ten at dusk.

Our deepest sorrow,

Dr. James Engintasick.

I wasn't . . . . wasn't pregnant. My hands started to shake and the tears started falling without my knowledge. I fell to my knees and shrieked. I didn't want to get up from where I was, I didn't want to see the world ever again. I couldn't imagine how I was going to tell Lucas this. I could just imagine how his face would go from really happy to heartbroken in an instant. I wanted so much to die.

The pain that entered my body was at an all-time high. I didn't care if Dad was home or not, all I cared about was my baby didn't exist. It was nothing, just a thing that passed. I could hear my dad coming downstairs with his face strung up.

"Katie, I know."

I looked up at him. He had a phone in his hand and he looked like he did when Mom died. I was confused, but didn't say anything. I was too ashamed to speak. I felt like crap.

"I'm sorry. I know you liked him."

I looked at him again. He sat next to me and held me. I didn't know what to say, so I just held back.

"We'll go and see him tomorrow. Okay, princess?"

"Wait. What are you talking about?"

The look on his face was scaring me more than ever. I knew he was talking about Lucas but I didn't know what he was talking about. I had just seen him, he was fine.

"I . . . thought you knew. Sweetie, Lucas got into an accident tonight. His car was hit, and the car sped off. He's at the hospital now."

I doubled up and looked at his face again. He wasn't lying. I ran out of the house and to my car. I struggled with my keys and pulled out of the drive and headed off for St. Cathy's. I tried hard to focus on the road and it took all of my energy. It didn't help that the rain came crashing down on my windshield.

I ran into the hospital and up to the front desk.

"Warren!" I demanded.

The nurse looked at me, confused.

"Excuse me?"

"Warren, Lucas Warren! Is he here?"

"I'm sorry, but do you know him?"

"I . . . ." I thought about this for a second. "I'm his girlfriend."

She nodded and told me he was in surgery. I was directed to the area where I could watch and I looked down at him. He was sedated and he wasn't responding to the medication. I couldn't stop crying. Then I heard the sound of the flat line, and all I could do was shout.

"LUCAS!"

Time and time again the doctor's tried, and time and time again they failed. Then they stopped and called it off.

Lucas Warren, the boy I fell in love with, was dead.

Land of Misfit Dreams

My eyes opened slowly. I had no idea what happened or where I was. I sat up slowly and saw my car in a tangled mess. I looked around but no one was even close to me. They were all huddled around this other person. I got up off of the ground and stumbled over to them, only to realize that they were huddled around . . . . *me.* I gasped and tried to get someone's attention.

"Excuse me, but what's happening?"

He didn't answer; he didn't even look my way. I tried again to get his attention.

"Hey, what's going on here?"

Still, nothing. Nothing changed about his gaze towards the body that lay on the ground. I went to grab him but my hand just went through his body like I was a ghost. Was I? No one was even looking my way. I was about to give up when a voice spoke behind me.

"They can't hear you."

I turned around to see a man, standing on the road with his hands in his jacket pockets. He had grey eyes, like me. Sandy blonde hair, like me. I didn't know him, but my curiosity got the better of me.

"Who-who are you?"

"Come on, Luke. You don't know your old man?"

I took a sharp breath and stepped up to him, standing at eye level. He smiled kindly, and grabbed me to hug me.

"I missed you so much, son."

I was in awe and shock at the same time. I hugged him back, and teared up when I finally said the words I had longed so say for eighteen years.

"I missed you too, Dad."

We walked down that road for a good twenty minutes, talking about everything that he had missed. He told me he was sorry for what he had done to my mother, and that he had taken his own life. He was sorry for missing out on my life, and never being there for me. I assured him that I wasn't upset at him. I was just glad I got to meet him. Got to finally have an image of my father.

"So, Dad. Not that I enjoy talking with you but . . . where are we? Am I dead?"

He sighed and looked at me.

"No, Luke. You're not dead. You're in between. Limbo, as some people would call it."

"But, what are you-"

"I'm here to help you. Either you come with me or you go back. That decision falls entirely on you. So, what is it?"

I took a step back and thought about it. I couldn't give him a straight answer right now.

"I . . . . I don't know. There's this girl if I go back. But she's . . . . pregnant, with my kid. The thing is though, I don't know if the baby is mine. I slept with her last week I don't think she can be pregnant with my child."

"I see. Well Luke until you make a decision it looks like we're both stuck here."

I sighed and took a walk down Main. He looked around for a bit and asked me the one thing I knew he'd ask me.

"So, you a Northern boy now?"

I laughed and shook my head.

"Not even close. I'm in between; I only tolerate it because of two people."

"Who?"

"Well, my best friend Nicole. She was the first one to talk to me when I got here, although I and she haven't been on the best of terms lately and I guess the second girl is because of it."

"The girl that you might have impregnated?"

"Yeah. Katie." I guess the way I said her name let him ask his next question.

"Do you love her?"

I nodded, letting him see the seriousness in my eyes.

"I am. It scares me how much I am. The thing that I'm afraid of loving her. Because everyone in my life has left me in a terrible way. I don't want her to leave either."

"Luke, if you love her and you decide to come with me, you'd be leaving her."

"I know, but I don't want to leave you either."

"Luke I've been dead for eighteen years, I think I'd be fine."

"I know you'd be fine. I wouldn't."

"Luke your more of a man then I could ever hope to be. This girl needs you. Far more than I do."

I nodded and hugged him one more time.

"I love you so much, son. You'll always have me and you know it."

"I know, Dad. I love you too."

I felt my body tingling. I didn't know what was going on but all I knew was I was heading back.

I opened my eyes slowly and found myself in a hospital bed. Katie was sitting next to me, crying. I blinked and spoke.

"Why so sad, rich girl?"

She looked up and started crying more and kissed my forehead.

"I thought you left me, you stupid boy."

"Well, I came back. I came back to tell you I love you, and I'm not going anywhere ever again."

I kissed her and held her tightly. I was not leaving her, ever again.

Little White Lies

I woke up the next morning wishing that last night wasn't a dream. I didn't know whether or not if Lucas was actually awake or if my mind wanted me to have a sane night's rest. I looked over at him and he was sleeping, so I'm guessing the latter happened. I sighed and went to go get some coffee when his voice sliced through me.

"Cream, no sugar."

I smiled and turned around. His grey eyes were barley open but he was breathing and smiling at me. I nodded and blew him a quick kiss. I left the room and bumped into Nicole. The sight of her was a total wreck. Her hair was everywhere, she had been crying nonstop from the look of it, and her glasses were crooked.

"Nicole, are you okay?" I asked.

"Like you even care. Move I have to see Lucas."

I let her pass and went to the cafe. I didn't know why she was still so upset. I don't like what I did to her but I can't take it back. She should move past it. I poured my coffee and sat down for a minute 'cause I didn't want to run into Luke and Nicole together. I didn't mind that they were best friends, nor did I mind that Nicole had come to visit him. What I minded was the fact that she is so quick to judge me when she knows of the history that I and she have. She knows that she's done some pretty horrific things herself. But those are her skeletons to deal with, I accept my demons.

What I was most concerned about was telling Luke that I wasn't pregnant. His reaction has played over and over in my mind for a few hours and it's been a mixed reaction every time I've played it out. Sometimes it's a good reaction and he is happy, but others it's not pretty.

I got up and walked out of the cafe with Lucas' coffee in my hand. I decided to take a little walk to figure out how to tell him this. He's been so good to me that I don't want him to feel like he did something wrong when he's done everything right. He shouldn't have this to deal with, not now at least.

I found myself at the nursery. Looking at all of the children I began to cry again. That pain and that empty feeling shot back up and it pained me so much to know that I wasn't pregnant. But what hurt more was that small part that was glad to know that I wasn't. I think that was what hurt the most. The fact that there is a part of me that is happy for me not being pregnant really hurts.

I wiped my tears and headed for Luke's room. Along the way I tried to find ways to tell him the truth but with each time I did I grew more and unhappy with them. I knew what I had to do.

I smiled and went inside his room. Nicole was gone so I had him to myself for now. I kissed him and lay on his bed with him. I knew he'd ask, so when he did I knew what I was going to say.

"Hey, how's the baby?"

I looked up at him and smiled, kissing him one more time.

"Fine, the baby is just fine."

One little white lie won't hurt.

What Doesn't Kill You Makes You Angrier

I was so happy today. My rehab begins and I'm more then excited to get out of this bed. It's been about three days since my accident but from what I'm hearing it wasn't such an accident. I was able to get a copy of the police report and it clearly states in three separate paragraphs that this was a hit and run. Someone tried to kill me and the only person that came to mind was the one guy who couldn't stand me, John Albright.

It was clear in my mind that he was the kind of person to try to run another person off of the road and get away with it, because after all he was the "football god". He could do no wrong, and when he did everyone just looked the other way. I couldn't believe no one has done a thing to stop him and ask him what he was doing that night. I tried telling Katie what I thought, but she rebuffed me.

"Luke, he was at his party. You know that."

"He could've easily left and-"

"Luke, John may be a lot of things but he's not that. He didn't try to kill you. No one knows who did, but we're trying everything."

"Katie I know this sounds crazy but trust me."

"Lucas I love you but this is too crazy. Just let it go, you need to focus on getting better. Please for me just get better."

I sighed, knowing my attempt as all for not. I let it go but I knew in the back of my head that John was the one that tried to kill me. The mere thought of it made me so angry I couldn't wait to get out of this bed and get my hands on him. For one I still owe him for sleeping with Nicole and now this. John is going to rue the day he tried to kill me.

I took a step and the immediate pain rushed into my body. I cringed and tried with all of my might not to cry. I was about ready to give up when my father's voice went through my head.

"You can do this, Luke."

It was with that voice I knew that this was easy. I grunted and put one foot in front of the other, ignoring the unbearable pain shooting through my legs and spine. I knew that I could do it, after my entire name is Lucas Jonathan Warren. I could do anything.

The rehab passed quickly so I could go home early but with one condition, I sit out on five games and do limited workouts. I accepted without even fighting. Walter made sure if I didn't accept it then my season was done. I wanted that state title so bad so I had to accept.

As I lay down in my bed I took some time to figure out what I was going to do next. I got visitors, mostly friends from the team. Katie stays as long as she can, which makes me happier then I should be. She makes everything better and to tell you the truth I'm excited to have a pregnant girlfriend. It doesn't matter that I'm not the father; I was going to be there for her for this.

And as for John, he hasn't killed me. I was going to get to the bottom of this.

Even if it kills me.

Back to Our Real Lives

It's already Monday? I was so caught up in Luke's accident I had lost track of the days. I woke up and heaved myself from the hospital chair, and tried my best to remain quiet so Lucas can sleep. But I guess in the middle of my changing he awoke. He smiled at me and let out a low whistle.

"Very funny, Luke. Go back to sleep."

"How can I sleep when my girl looks so damn sexy without a top on?"

"Well do good with rehab today and you might just get her in your bed tonight."

He laughed and brought me to him.

"You know I love you, Katie Earnwright. I love you so much."

I smiled and put my hand on his heart, feeling the soft beat of it against me.

"I love you too, Lucas Warren."

I kissed him softly and put my shirt on, to Lucas' dismay. I kissed him again and left the room promising him that I'd be back after school. I walked out into the sunlight up to my car. I was about to get in when John stopped me.

"How is he?" He asked.

"Why do you care?"

"I do, more then you know."

I walked away from him and didn't bother listening to him as he tried to call me back. I just wanted to get to school and forget I ever talked to John.

I got to school around twelve thirty and headed straight for fifth period. I was so late I couldn't get my make-up work so I just went to my desk and stayed quiet for the whole class. I ignored all the stares I got from everyone. I guess John must have started a rumor about me and Luke. Great, as if my life wasn't so screwed up as it is. I left out of class early so I could use the bathroom.

I was just getting ready to leave when I overheard Nicole in the next stall, crying.

"Nicole?'

Her crying stopped automatically and she must have wiped her tears.

"What do you want, Katie?"

"I just wanted to see how you were doing."

"Obviously not great."

"Well anytime you want to talk . . ."

"I'll pass thanks."

I sighed and walked out of the restroom. I was not enjoying my day and on top of it I had cheer practice after school. I wonder if I can skip for just one night, and go see Luke.

I endured the rest of the day and got in my car. I didn't even think twice about it. I drove up to the hospital and walked into Luke's room. He looked at me and smiled.

"You should be at practice."

"You should be too."

He laughed and I went to sit on his bed.

"You know what I found out today? My old life, cheerleading, friends and all of it . . . . they don't mean as much to me as you do. I love you, Luke. You are my life now."

I kissed him and held his hand up to my chest. I was ready to spend my life with him.

I got up out of bed and closed his door, ready to see if he can use all of his muscles yet.

The Return

I woke up late on Tuesday. I wasn't supposed to; because today was the day I get to return to school. One of the best things about being in a car accident is that for a while everyone just looks the other way when you do something stupid. I sat up and got dressed slowly. I was still pretty banged up and the only reason I get to leave today is my coach and my mom. Both of them want me to return to school, maybe for different reasons but all the same I was going back.

I left my room and went to go see my doctor. He told me the only reason I was let go was because I was showing signs of recovery ten times faster than the average car crash victim. He says it's my physical attributes, but I think it's my motivation. My motivation to be a father was all I needed.

The idea of me being a father started growing on me. It made me think of my father, who took his own life because of his own heartbreak. I wanted to be the father that he couldn't be. The whole prospect made my entire outlook on life change, as well as my relationship with Katie. You just can't understand the love I have for her. Who knows what my anger would've led me to do if I didn't meet her.

My thinking left me in a daze and I found myself in the car with Walter, and ever since the accident he's been a little tougher.

"If you wouldn't have been with that girl, Luke, you wouldn't be near dead."

"Good morning to you too, Walter."

"Look Luke, I think Katie is great. I do, but ever since you two have been dating you've been all over the map."

"I was all over the map before I was dating her."

"Well you need to focus on things that matter rather than a girlfriend. Like school, keep your mindset on school because you're behind in your work."

"I know, don't worry about me. I'll be fine."

He grunted and pulled over at the school, letting me out. I closed the door and looked around. No one was outside during the day so the school just looked empty. I walked in and signed a few forms in the main office and made my way to class.

Say what you want about me, but I got some looks of compassion from plenty of people. I avoided anyone from the football them including John. I knew he had something to say about me being out for six games. So, to avoid any and all insults, I hid in the bathroom until the end of the day. I'm a coward.

I saw Katie emerging from class and I walked up to her smiling, but her response wasn't what I thought it would be. She took one look at me and walked away. I stared at her until she was out of sight, and then sighed and went outside to wait for Walter.

This return sucks.

Revelations

I rushed home in such a hurry I actually forgot how I got there. I was just trying to get away from Lucas. I knew I had to tell him that I wasn't pregnant, but every time I tried I got caught up with making sure he was okay. I was just protecting him from more pain that he was already in. He will hate me forever, never speak to me again and I deserved it. I mean, who keeps a secret like that from the person you love? Just the sight of him today made me nervous about what I would have to do, so I didn't speak to him. I needed to convince myself I was ready to tell him the truth.

I called him on his cell and got his machine. I left him a message telling him to meet me at the field, so we could talk about some things. Mainly that he was not the father of my child. I didn't even have a child and that's what kills me the most. I know that if God blessed me with the chance to become a mother I would do the greatest job. I guess now was not that time.

I went up to my closet and looked for something to wear. I know it sounds cliché but I wanted to look my best for him, even if I knew that I would break his heart. Everything I do now it's with Lucas in mind. He makes my world turn and now I have to prepare for the worst. It's going to be rough without him but I can't keep this lie up anymore. I never meant to lie it's just that he was just in a hit and run. I needed to keep him from this pain. I knew I had to tell him sooner or later. I would have gone with later, though.

Leaving my house, I felt like I was leaving it for prison on death row. Luke was going to be so angry with me and I know I deserve it but he needs to understand my side of the story. He needs to know I did it out of love with no intention to hurt him.

I turned onto Eastgate High Road and circled the parking lot a few times and finally parked at the gates to the field. I sat at one of the tables outside and waited for Luke to come. He still wasn't able to drive so Walter would have to bring him.

I was so nervous I was shaking. I couldn't concentrate on anything else. I sat the tow truck turn onto the road and almost threw up.

Luke limped my way with a smile, my smile, just for me. It made it even harder for me to say what I needed to say. I couldn't look at him without crying. He rushed over to me and held me and whispered.

"What's wrong, Katie?"

I looked at him up and down and sobbed out the lie that I had kept from him.

"Luke . . . . I lied. I'm not pregnant. I got the results on the night of your accident and I didn't want to tell you because I wanted to spare you more pain. Luke, please I'm so sorry."

He looked at me, and didn't say a word. He got up, and without even saying a thing to me went back to the tow truck and got in. In that moment I knew in my heart what had happened.

Lucas broke up with me.

Tears Don't Fall

I couldn't think. I couldn't talk. All I could do was tear up. But I refused to let them fall. I didn't cry when my parents died, I won't cry now. Walter knew that something was up so he didn't say much which was good because I didn't know what I'd say. I just didn't know anymore. It was like being crushed, having everything good in your life taken away.

Katie, the girl I was falling more and more in love with, lied to me about being pregnant. She told a lie right to my face. I can't understand it. Once again, I refuse to cry. It's not who I am.

We got home and I went up to my room. I sat and looked at my jersey, and how if I had the chance to go back and not accept the offer by Coach, would I be where I am now? No, because if it wasn't for that game I wouldn't have had sex with Katie. I just couldn't believe this, how could she do this to me? Why, why now?

Looking around I began to notice that my life had changed dramatically and I didn't know if it was a good thing. All I knew was that my girlfriend lied to me about having a baby. I didn't know whether or not to forgive that. My mind was blank, I felt sick and I wanted so much to cry but my damn pride kept getting in the way.

So here I am, alone in my room with a broken heart and a bruised pride. Why does this hurt so much? I feel like dying, this hurts worse than my real injuries. A car crash has nothing on a broken heart.

My phone rang, making me jump. It was Katie. I hit ignore and laid down. My life once had meaning, and now I don't know weather or not if it's worth it. I just want to lay down and shut the world away.

I turned on my mp3 and listened to every love song I could find before finally at long last I found it. Tears Don't Fall by Bullet For My Valentine. I related to this in every way humanly possible. Every time I tried to think of something else, Katie keeps popping into mind like a bullet.

This could not hurt any worse, but then I think about football and she keeps coming back into focus. I had this song on repeat and as it played for the fourth time in a row my pride finally broke. The tears fell down my face like a rainstorm and I didn't even bother let them stop. This pain was far too much for me to bear. Forget school, forget football. All I knew was that if I cried over a girl one of two things was certain.

I knew we were not meant to be.

Or I was so in love with her it hurts to be away.

Either way, I'm crying.

Butterfly

I decided to walk home because one with the tears that were propelling down my face I would crash without a doubt. The other reason was because I needed to think. I needed to process what had just happened. Lucas went off in such a hurry that I couldn't even think of words to say to him to get him to stop. My car will be fine, it's in my parking space with a camera right over. Anyone who would be stupid enough to try and steal it, hey it won't be my funeral.

I feel so bad for what I did. In my head it all seemed to make sense. Tell Lucas after a few weeks of rehab and he'll forgive me. But the way it went in my head, I was happy. Right now I feel terrible.

Eastgate seemed so far from my house. Western Ave. was about five blocks away from the school but with how I feel it seems like it's fifteen miles. I never felt this kind of pain in my life, not even after John broke up with me.

Compared to this John felt like a summertime fling, it didn't matter once fall hit. Losing Luke, who's been nothing but sweet and understanding with me, hurts almost as much as when I lost my mother.

I was on Main when I felt the raindrops. The spring was never calm with us. It was always rainy or sunny. Nothing else was an option. I walked near the hospital, just off of Main. I had an appointment tomorrow but with everything right now pouring onto me I wanted to see if I could move it to today.

"I'm here to see Dr. Reynolds." I said to the nurse at the front desk. She checked her computer.

"He will be right with you, please have a seat."

I smiled and took a seat next to a bunch of old magazines. I looked through them but none got to me. At this point I don't think anything could peak my curiosity, except for maybe Lucas. But since I know that that's impossible, I threw the magazines back into their pile and waited for the doctor to get here.

"Katie!" A voice said.

I looked up and saw my doctor smiling at me. I stood up and shook his hand.

"Hey, Dr. Reynolds."

He smiled and led me to his office and sat me down. He took off his white coat and sat in his chair.

"So, I wasn't supposed to see you until tomorrow. Is everything okay?"

"Yeah . . . . well no. You said I was a strange case and well . . . I just broke up with my boyfriend so the walk I took led me here. So I just wanted to know what made my case so out of the ordinary."

"Okay, well I took a look at your blood work and noticed that you've been stressed since the beginning of the spring. What happened?"

"Well me and John broke up . . . . and I met Lucas."

"And you slept with Lucas?"

I nodded.

"Well Katie, the reason you missed your period was because you were stressed. Also because of whatever has been going on with you and Lucas. Everything piled into one mind tends to take it's toll on the body."

Everything he said made sense. Not more then a few weeks after me and John break up, I got with Lucas. As I listened to Dr. Reynolds talk, I began to realize that I didn't take my time in getting over John. John was my everything since freshman year, and when he left me I wasn't myself. I was angry at everything. I saw Luke as my excuse which made me feel worse because I used him. Nicole was right. I was a bad person.

I thanked Dr. Reynolds and left. I went down Main and turned left onto Western. I opened my front door and looked for Dad. Of course he wasn't home. I went up to my room and laid on my bed. Sometimes my dad calls me his butterfly because I was always so pure and gentle. Right now I felt like a spider, full of venom and at the slightest threat I bite.

Luke didn't deserve to be used like I used him.

All I can hope is that he forgives me.

Fat chance.

Not the American Average

I woke up late today. I wasn't in any rush. I was still off of the team for a good week. We were winning though. Since our loss to Trenton, we won the last four games bringing our record to 5-1. We had four more games and I was allowed to suit up for the next one but I get no playing time. After this game they will have me do some workouts to see if I'm ready for play the next week. We were up against North Orchard so we would more than likely go 6-1. If we win six we automatically qualify for the playoffs. The playoffs are just two games since most of the teams finish with the same records. The teams who win that game go to the state championship.

I heaved myself out of bed and limped to my bathroom. I turned on the light and started the shower. I stood there for about a good twenty minutes before I did anything. I was still hung-over off of losing the one girl I ever cared about.

Katie . . . . how did this all happen? How did we go from hating each other, falling in love, and then not even talking to each other? She stopped calling me around three in the morning, for all I assumed was that she was tired. I wanted so much to call her back but my pride got in my way. She means everything to me but I was not sure if I could forgive her for what she had done. She *lied* about having a child, my child. The only possible reason was her excuse for not wanting me in more pain. It hurts to say this, but deep down she was right. That's what hurts the most, knowing that she is right in a way, because all I want is to blame her.

I walked downstairs to the kitchen. Walter was sitting at the table reading the newspaper and didn't notice when I took his bagel. Today was supposed to be a busy day at the shop, where I had to work until I got better. We were the only shop open on Sundays so we had the money coming in. Walter doesn't believe in the seventh day of rest I guess.

"Luke, did you empty out the oil drums?" he asked.

"Yeah, they're in your truck. I was hoping I could get them filled first thing today."

"That's fine. Just make sure you have enough energy for the engines."

"I will."

I went back to my room and got my work vest. As I left I heard Katie's ringtone on my phone. I looked at her picture and threw my phone on my bed. I won't need it today. We got in his truck and headed for the corner of Main and Lion road. Our first customer didn't show up so we did some busy work around the garage.

It wasn't until four that she came. Katie drove her little car into the garage and got out. I walked into the office and got the papers, and came back out and bumped into her. I looked into her eyes and almost about poured myself on her. I held back everything and handed her the papers. She signed them and avoided my look, turning around and walking towards her car.

I wanted so much to chase her, hold her and tell her that everything would be okay. But as I watched her pull away and out of sight one thing ran through my mind.

She lied, and that can never be forgiven. I would never ever again have Katie Earnwright in my arms.

For now, that was good enough for me.

The Memory Remains

My alarm clock blared into my head and jolted me out of bed. I sat up and groaned. I knew today was game day; I just didn't want it to be. Call me depressed but these last few days have been . . . . not great. It's going to be tough to try act all peppy and cheery today. Not only that but I have to see Lucas again, and seeing him hurts me every time. I knew he didn't want to talk to me, but I can't give up on us. I know if we try, we can make it.

After my shower I got dressed and headed downstairs. Dad was sitting at the table with a shocked look on his face so I decided to play daughter and ask what was wrong but before I could he spoke.

"When were you going to tell me?"

I stopped dead in my tracks and looked at the table. My pregnancy test papers were in front of him.

"Dad I-"

"What? You what? You were going to tell me? When? When your stomach got to the size of a watermelon?"

"Dad, I'm not pregnant. I checked. It's on that paper you read!"

"Katie that's not the point! My point is that you're eighteen, and too young and invested in school to be doing this kind of thing!"

I stood there and took it. It was only until he mentioned Mom that I said something.

"Did you even think about your mother?"

"Did I think about Mom? I ALWAYS think about Mom, do you? When you're at the office telling people that their dreams can't come true because they don't meet YOUR requirements, do you think of Mom?"

He stared at me, open mouthed and shocked. I used this to my advantage and turned to leave. I didn't bother with saying I love you to him because sometimes to be honest I don't. I was never fond of his career choice or his method of making money. We got rich off of the broken dreams in this town, and it hurts me to think that he doesn't care.

I got into my car and pulled out of my driveway. Out of the corner of my eye I saw someone in a red hoodie watching me with his hood up. I shook my head and made my way to school.

My first three classes seemed pretty normal; I didn't have Luke until fifth hour. But something told me that today wasn't going to be a normal day.

As soon as that thought ran through my mind, the alarm went off.

Then, as if piercing through the air, a gunshot.

Hide and Seek

I woke up a little after six in the morning. Monday already? Damn, I thought it was Saturday. I guess I should be excited after all I get to return to the field this week. I slowly got dressed and heaved myself out of bed not wanting to go and see Katie and have my heart get Muai Thai kicked again. Something about today didn't click, and I didn't know how to call it.

I was finally able to walk properly and my driving rights were still on the fritz but I got to use the tow truck today to get to school due to Walter fully employing me at the garage. I went downstairs and saw Walter and Christiana talking quietly and after seeing me come in, they shut up and went back to breakfast. I avoided their looks and opened the fridge. It was only after I poured my glass of orange juice that Walter finally spoke.

"Luke, how are you feeling?"

I shrugged. "Okay, I guess. Little nervous for practice."

His silence prompted me to turn around and look at him.

"What's going on, Walter?"

He cleared his throat and looked at me with cold eyes.

"Luke, we don't want you playing football anymore."

I wanted to laugh, but his voice and how he said it stopped me. I looked at Christina and her face was glaring at the tablecloth. I shook my head and looked back at Walter.

"Why?"

"We . . . we just don't want you to get hurt anymore. Luke you're too important to us to lose."

"Walter I'm not going to die playing football."

"How do you know that? Did God tell you?"

"Look I-"

"No you look! I care about you too much to lose you! Now what you're going to do is after school is talk to the coach and get you off the team! Do you understand?"

I didn't answer. I just grabbed my bag and left. The drive will help me clear my head and hopefully calm me down. How dare he say I can't play anymore? It's my life and it's my choice. I turned onto Eastgate Drive and parked in my place.

On my way into the school I noticed Kurt Gregory, one of my classmates, enter the school rather quickly. He was an unusual person and never really talked much. He did however suffer from John and his boys tormenting him, and from what I hear it's been going on since junior high.

I went inside and to my locker. First hour already started so I was late but I didn't care. I made my way to my class when all of a sudden the alarm went off. Probably just a drill or something.

But as soon as that happened I heard the screaming and then, like a whip cracking through the air, a gunshot.

Drops of Jupiter

We really didn't know how to react until a teacher came in and told us to get down and turn off all the lights. I instantly bolted down next to Jennifer, my friend from the squad. We looked at each other and our expressions were the same. We didn't know what the hell was going on.

All I could think of was Lucas and if he was okay. My next thought was who could've done this, and how it was possible. We didn't have security guards so it was easy to just waltz right in with a gun, but I didn't know of anyone with enough of a motive to harm anyone in this school. I mean sure we have bullying but it's not like we're Columbine or something.

I looked over and saw a few kids I didn't know crying in a corner, and I whispered as softly as I could to them.

"Why are you crying?"

The girl wiped her tears and looked at me.

"I didn't think he was serious! We thought he was joking!"

"Who?"

"Kurt! Kurt's the one with the gun!"

"Kurt who?"

She glared at me. "I don't expect you to know! He's not popular like you!"

I looked down and played with the dirt on the floor.

"He's our friend, not that you care."

I looked back at them and then looked away. Part of me wanted to cry and part of me wanted to yell at them for judging me so harshly without taking the time to get to know me. But as I thought that, I never really took the time to get to know them either. So it's a two way street that I don't want to go down.

I looked back at Jennifer and started talking to her.

"So, do you think that the game will be canceled tonight?"

She looked at me with confusion. "Katie, its Monday."

I was shocked. I didn't know that. I was really not myself lately, and it was starting to show. I sat under my table and started to tear up a little. I was completely heartless to everyone. I never told Dad I loved him, I lost Luke and now this. I was so pathetic that I didn't know what day it was.

All of a sudden the door opened and everyone screamed at once but we quickly shut up when it was John and . . . *Lucas*. I looked at both of them and they both looked at me. We knew we had to stay in the same room with each other now and it was killing the three of us.

"Luke! Are you okay?" I asked.

"Yeah, I was heading to class when I heard the shot and I ran into John here. We decided to look for you when he told me you had this class."

I looked at John, who was avoiding my stare. I knew that in some way or another, these two cared for me. Even if it meant risking their lives to see if I was alright.

I looked back at Luke and knew in my heart that he did love me.

If was the last time I would see him, I know at least that much.

Fade to Black

I looked out of the door window to see if anyone was coming. I looked over at the people in the room and I saw Katie, sitting in a corner and crying, John was standing on my other side and everyone else was bunched away. The girl who was sobbing looked over at John and spoke.

"You . . . you caused all of this! Why couldn't you just leave him alone?"

John looked both shocked and ashamed. "I didn't know he would bring a gun into the school."

"But he did! ALL because you couldn't leave him alone!"

"Look let's not argue over who caused this okay?" I blurted in.

John and the girl looked over at me.

"All we need to do is sit this out," I said. "I'm going to go out and see if the coast is clear."

"Luke, no!" Katie said. I looked over at her and couldn't help but tear up.

"Luke, you can't leave. Someone is out there with a gun."

I walked over to her and put my head against hers.

"I promise if we both make it through this we'll talk okay?"

She nodded and let me go but before I could leave John grabbed my arm.

"I'm coming with you, Luke." He said.

I saw the look in his eyes and it was one of fear. I had never seen fear in his eyes before.

"Well then let's go."

I took one last look at Katie and left, with John following right behind me. We turned right, into the senior hallway where our lockers were. We didn't know what to expect or where this guy was but every noise made us jump. I looked over at John and he was slowly following me with the greatest of ease. All of a sudden a voice stopped us both.

"Turn around."

We did as he said and there he was, Kurt Gregory. Gun in one hand, bag in the other.

"Kurt, what are you doing man?" I asked.

He looked at me and smirked.

"What the fuck does it look like I'm doing, Luke?"

"Why-why?"

"Why? You want to know why? Why don't you ask the piece of shit standing next to you why! All the years of doing his homework, taking his shit, him dunking my head into every toilet of the school last year! Or how about the time he and a group of his friends kicked my ass Homecoming week. You look at him and you ask why I'm doing all of this!"

I looked over at John who was shaking and crying a little bit. I looked back at Kurt who had his gun aimed at me.

"Whoa, Kurt. What are you doing man?"

"You ruined my life too, Luke. I was supposed to get on the football team, not you! I was supposed to be the popular one, NOT YOU!"

I started at him with disbelief. He continued on with his speech.

"I tried to end it a few weeks ago. I hoped you died in that car wreck! But no! You just had to live, DIDN'T YOU?!?!?"

It hit me hard. John was innocent. He didn't try to kill me that night, Kurt did.

"And now, I'm going to kill both of the guys that ruined my life!"

In a flash John bolted at Kurt, grabbing the gun and trying to shake it loose from him. They circled around with both hands on the gun when all of a sudden a shot fired.

Then another.

I opened my eyes, and both Kurt Gregory and John Albright were lying on the hallway floor, covered in their own blood.

Running Up That Hill

My ears were piercing right now. We had just heard two gunshots and I knew someone I cared about was hurt, or worse dead. I couldn't stop thinking that someone I knew was gone. Weather it was Luke or John, I knew it. But I also knew we couldn't just sit here and wait to die, we had to get out of here.

"Listen, we have to get out of here. We can go the other way." I said.

"Are you insane?" A person demanded. "There is someone with a gun out there!"

I looked over at the group of kids crying in a corner and looked back at him.

"Well according to these guys it's only one guy. So we need to get out of here."

He looked at me like I was crazy. I didn't care; all I cared about was getting out of this school alive. I wanted to see my dad. I wanted to see Luke. I just didn't want to die.

We got out of the room one by one with me in the front of the pack. We were on the second floor and the first set of stairs was close to us, so we were close to an exit. The only problem is that all the exits are programmed during an emergency to set an alarm off when they open so either the shooter would hear us or the cops would assume we were in on the shooting and would take us down. The later didn't seem so bad.

We got to the exit and I turned to look at the group when I saw someone carrying a body. I took a second look and noticed that the person alive was Luke . . . . and the person he was carrying was . . . . my stomach dropped and my heart exploded . . . he was carrying John. I didn't make a noise and led everyone out the door. The alarm went off and we were met with guns from about five SWAT members. We were safe, but Luke was still inside with John's body. Inside my mind I prayed that John would be alright.

I was led to an ambulance to see if I was hurt. I was in shock but I was fine. I just couldn't believe that someone was in so much pain to actually bring a gun into school. Who could be in such emotional duress to decide to kill somebody? The mere thought brought tears to my eyes.

Dad's voice was the only thing that calmed me down, and he saw me out of the crowd of kids in the street.

"KATIE!" He shouted.

I looked up. His face was full of fear and relief that I was okay. He got to me and pulled me to him and all I could do was cry. I cried for happiness, I cried for fear, but above all I cried because I was okay.

Something told me John wasn't.

You're Guardian Angel

I couldn't move. I couldn't think. All I saw was John, laying there in a pool of his own blood and next to him was Kurt, holding the gun and dead. My thoughts were completely and utterly blank. I looked around and saw that I was alone. I moved over to John and shook him but he was unresponsive. I picked him up and slowly made my way to the end of the hall where we were before Kurt stopped us.

I found an exit but it was barricaded with desks and chairs. I turned and went towards the end of the hall. There was an exit there, but it was blocked off too. I cursed under my breath and walked to the front of the school and saw it wasn't blocked off. I opened the door with my foot and was met with guns and shouting. They quickly lowered their weapons and picked John up from my arms and led me to an ambulance.

As I was being examined a few cops and reporters questioned me but I didn't say anything. I was too upset. I looked to the east and saw Katie with her father and I breathed a huge sigh of relief. I was so worried that she would be hurt. I looked around at the fear and the shock everyone had on their face. Eastgate was not the place for this kind of thing to happen, until today.

I was released and went looking for Walter and found him by the spirit rock.

"Dad!" I shouted.

He turned and burst into tears and held me.

"I was afraid I'd lose you son. I'm so sorry."

"It's okay. I'm okay."

His grip went away and at his side was Christina. She couldn't stop crying and held me longer then Walter had. I held her tightly and didn't let go until I almost lost my breath.

"It's okay, Mom. It's okay. I'm fine."

"You-you don't ever leave without saying goodbye, do you understand me?"

I smiled. "Yes, Mom."

I told them I had to go see John and they gave me a lift to the hospital. I got there and off the bat they told me he was in surgery. I waited for three hours, pacing back and forth.

It was about five hours after surgery as I sat in his room did he finally wake up. His voice sounded rough and his eyes were hazy.

"You didn't have to stay."

I looked up and smiled at him.

"You didn't have to save me"

He laughed, or at least tried too.

"Look, Luke. I'm . . . I'm sorry. For everything. You came from out of nowhere and I felt threatened. It's just . . . . all I knew was football and Katie, and I saw I was losing both. Football to you, Katie because of myself. My only regret is treating you like crap."

I couldn't speak, and I looked at the floor.

"Anyway, I don't think I'm going to make it out of this, so could you do me a favor?"

I nodded.

"In my pocket is a note for Katie. I was going to give it to her today, make sure she gets it."

I went inside his pocket and found a folded piece of yellow paper. I didn't look at it long, because I heard him breathing slower and slower until finally at nine thirty-two his heart finally gave out.

I walked out of his room to find Katie waiting outside of it. She looked at me and knew that it was true, and even as she held me it felt even worse.

John Albright was dead.

My Immortal

I sat on my bed with a box of tissues and John's note. I've read it every day for three weeks and still his words have not escaped me. I looked over it one more time:

Katie,

I know that my words mean nothing when I say them. But perhaps when I write them you will feel more inclined to listen. I understand the pain I put you through. The pain that you feel does not overshadow how much you meant to me over the last three years. When I first met you you've made my life complete, and with every day that we spent together I felt more and more like a human being, like I belonged. You passion and your faith kept me alive when my home life brought me down. Even now as I write this I tear up with the thoughts and memories of our past life. But they must remain that, memories. I have been going down a dark road and with it cost me the one thing that made me happy, you. You have every single reason to hate me, and every single reason to never talk to me again. But on the off chance that you can one day forgive me, please know that I never stopped loving you. My love for you will never die. You will remain in my heart for the rest of my life. I know you love Lucas, and I won't stand in your way of being in a relationship with him. You may read this and think I'm just saying words to make you happy but

I mean every word I'm writing. Starting today, I will no longer be the guy everyone hates. I'm going to become the person you once thought I could be.

Not for you, but for me. I must prove to myself that I can be capable of loving someone as much as I have loved you. You may not see me after graduation, so while I still have the chance, I wish to say goodbye.

With love, sorrow, and regret,

John.

I looked over it again. And again before I put it down. It's only been three weeks since the shooting and everyone is still in a daze. I have not seen Lucas since the hospital and my guess was that he and his family left for a few weeks. He wasn't answering his phone and his foster dad closed the garage. The football team lost the last three games via forfeit and the game this Friday was going to be the first one we've had since.

I got out of bed and looked at the pictures that I got from his funeral. He was so happy, and so in love with life in them. I was in some of them and when we were in the same picture he was smiling and laughing. Something in him changed and he lashed out on everyone. But the person who felt the sting was him. The words in his note were the words of the John I used to know. That John, I'll carry in my heart forever.

The funeral was somber. His dad flew in out of town for it and his mom was a complete wreck. They were on opposite sides of the rows and didn't even look at each other. It made me cringe with anger. At least make an attempt to get along for your sons' sake.

My dad didn't bring up the pregnancy issue after that. He assumed it was best for me to move on and not say a word. I understood, but I wish I had someone to talk too. It was killing me, being alone. Because being alone made me think of how much John used to mean to me and how much I still loved him. He meant the world to me and when he left me all I had were broken memories and painful thoughts.

I sat back down on my bed and looked through old photo albums of me and John over the years. However much I hated him for hurting me, there was always a part of me that still cared for him and wished that he would change. It's just that his change was too late. He was gone now and all I had of him were photos. Photos of a better time.

"Katie?" My dad called.

I got up and opened the door.

"Yeah, Dad?"

"Dinner is on the table."

"Okay."

Dad had stayed home from the office ever since the shooting. He's cooked dinner every day and it really felt like we were a family again.

I went downstairs and sat down. He gave me my drink and sat down.

"So, any luck with Luke?"

I looked down at my plate. "No."

"I'm sure he misses you."

"I know. I just wish he were here."

He looked at me and held my hand.

"You know, when they told me that you were in the school . . . I thought I lost you. And it made me think of your mother, and how much I miss her. I thought I was going to lose you too."

I started to tear up and listened.

"I know now that you love Luke, and I want you to know that I'm okay with it. I just want you to be happy."

I nodded and kissed him on the cheek. The tears were flowing and my heart was racing. I wanted this part of my dad for so long. It felt good to be embraced by the man who gave me love instead of giving me heartache.

We talked at the table long after dinner was done. We laughed, we joked, and we kissed and made up.

We were a family again.

The Music of the Night

Walter pushed me awake.

"Luke, come on we just landed."

I groaned and sat up from my seat on the plane. We left Germany a while ago and I needed my sleep. We went to see Nicole, who moved there a little after my accident. I missed her, and I loved seeing her but I was itching to get back to Eastgate. From what I heard we were 5-4, we lost our last three via forfeit. It didn't upset me as much as it made me excited to get back. We win this last game and we're in. If we lose, we say goodbye to the state title hopes.

We got off the plane and got our bags from the claim area. I was so dead tired I didn't even notice I was going the other way of my parents.

"Luke!" Christina called.

I turned around quickly. I laughed and walked back over to them. We got in the car and headed down seventy-five on the way home. I fell back asleep in the car until we got inside the town limits. I looked as we passed the school and saw the memorials that were placed there. I can't believe that John was gone, and even though we never saw eye to eye he still saved my life.

We turned onto Main and then took it all the way to Hawk, our street. It was amazing in Germany, but I missed this place so much. It was good to be home.

When I got inside I found my phone and found out Katie had called me at least four to five times. Before I went to go see her I promised myself I'd go to John's grave. I told myself since I was not at the funeral; I would be at his grave.

I drove up to Conquest Rd and pulled into the graveyard. I walked around until I found his grave and to be honest, it was surreal.

JOHNATHON FELIEX ALBRIGHT

1983-2012

Beloved son, friend, and athlete.

I sat down next to it and talked to him, like he were still here.

"Hey man. So, we've lost our last three games. Don't worry though, because everyone is so saddened over you they thought we shouldn't play. I know total bull crap right?"

The wind blew gently and made his flowers drop. I picked them up and leaned against his stone.

"So I know you're up there. Can you . . . . ," I paused. "Can you tell my dad I said hi? I miss him more and more every day. Just . . . . please be with us tomorrow. We want to win that state title for you. For coach, too."

I said my goodbyes and drove out. I was going to see Katie for the first time in a few weeks and I was nervous. Something told me she wanted us to be together tonight, but in actually I wanted to focus on football. I wanted John's memory to be a good one as we held up that state title trophy. I wanted nothing more. If I talk to her about it, maybe she would understand.

I turned on Western and saw that she was in her room. I took a deep breath and parked a few feet away so she wouldn't notice me. I stayed in the car and took another deep breath.

"You can do this, Luke." I said to myself.

So why am I so nervous?

Your Love is a Lie

As I lay in my bed, wondering if I had the influence to move, I got the strangest feeling I was going to be surprised today. I looked over at my clock. It was almost eight in the evening. I looked back up at my ceiling fan. I think today has been the most boring day of my life. I've barley paid attention in class, I'm due on almost every project, and cheerleading practice has been . . . . terrible.

I heaved myself up out of bed and sat at my desk. I went over the pictures of me and John for about the thousandth time and cried a little bit. God I miss him so much.

I heard the doorbell ring but I wasn't concerned. It's probably the guys from Dad's former office. He officially retired a few weeks ago and they've been hounding him nonstop to come back to the office. They don't understand that I need him, but all they care about is making a profit.

I heard footsteps on the stairs and thought nothing of it until I heard the knocking on my door. I got up and opened it and there he stood. Grey eyes, sandy blonde hair, and a gaze on his face that melted my heart and made me forget that I was sad. Luke was back.

I hugged him, gripping around his neck and releasing until I thought he was choking. I missed him so much and I took it upon myself to let him know.

"I missed you like crazy, Luke. How's Nicole?"

"She's uh, she's good. But I missed you too. More than you know and I think we need to talk."

I nodded and sat on my bed. I offered him a spot and sat quietly, letting him go on.

"Well, you know as well as I did, before me and John . . . . before we left I told you we'd talk . . . about us."

I smiled and rubbed my thighs slowly.

"Katie, I love you. You know that. You know I'd do anything for you. But I just . . . I can't be with you."

I was floored. It was like being kicked in the stomach so many times you felt like you had to vomit. I took a deep breath and spoke.

"You . . . don't want me?"

"No, it's not like that it's-"

"It sounds like that, Luke."

He paused and held my hand.

"Katie, John's death taught me that it's never too late to give up on something. I want to win that state championship so bad it keeps me up at night. I have to focus on football."

That stung. I made sure he felt the venom in my voice.

"Football? You don't want me . . . because of football. How stupid can you be honestly, Luke?"

"It's not stupid, and neither am I. I just want to focus on that for a while."

"So you abandon all hope for us strictly on the basis of football. This sounds like John, not Lucas."

"Katie, you lied to me about being pregnant!"

"To keep you from enduring more pain! I never asked to be not pregnant!"

"I never asked you TO be pregnant!"

"Well I never asked to fall in love with you but I did. Luke I hold you to a high standard because you're so much better than this. Don't give up on love for something as petty as sports."

"You don't get it do you? I saw John die. In that hallway and in that hospital room! He's gone because he tried to save me!"

"Don't you DARE play the guilt card with me Lucas Jonathon Warren! I miss John just as much as you do!"

"I wasn't trying to play the guilt card with you Katie! I want to make this up to John for saving me!"

"Luke, he didn't give a damn about you until he tried to save you. Why are you leaving a good thing with us for someone who never cared?"

"You know what, Katie? Maybe you just never got to know him."

"EXCUSE ME? I KNEW HIM MY WHOLE LIFE! I DATED HIM FOR THREE YEARS! DON'T YOU EVER SAY THAT TO ME AGAIN!"

He took a step back and put his arms up.

"I'm going to go."

"Fine, Luke! GO! You obviously never cared for me at all if you're just going to leave!"

He turned around and looked dead at me.

"Maybe I never did."

He turned around and closed my door.

With him, he took my heart.

Second Chances

Driving while I'm angry really never works out. I was too riled up to even think about driving. So much for trying to be civil with her. She needs to understand that when she lied to me about being pregnant, it put a hole through my heart so bad that it could have ended us for good. I love her but it's too much for me right now. That pain just doesn't go away.

I pulled into my driveway and went inside my house. Walter and Christina were out in town so I was all alone. It didn't really hurt me, but having someone to talk too might help. I flopped on my bed and went inside my pockets and found a piece of paper folded. It was Nicole's new number, so I got my phone out and dialed.

She answered on the third ring. "Hello?"

"Hey, Nicks."

"Hey, Luke! What's up?"

"Nothing. Well something happened with me and Katie."

"Uh oh . . . what happened this time?"

I told her everything. About the sex, about the pregnancy scare and about the fight we had. I was expecting her to take my side since we were best friends but I was wrong . . . to a point.

"Luke, I can understand not being sure about you two because of the scare . . . . but leaving her for football is stupid and you know it."

I sighed. "I know. I'm just afraid to tell her that I don't want to get hurt again."

"Luke, you are a wonderful person. You have a heart made of gold and don't ever forget that. So you're afraid of being hurt, who isn't? It's natural. You are going to be hurt; you're going to hurt others. It's life. You will break hearts and be heartbroken. You will make friends and enemies. Stop putting yourself on a pedestal. Don't make high expectations for yourself. Live your life the way it's meant to be for you and others will respond in their own way."

I smiled on the inside and shed a happy tear.

"Nicole you don't know how much you mean to me. I miss you every day and I wish you were here. I know Germany is where you belong and I'm happy for you. I just wish you were here, I need my best friend."

"Luke, I'm always a phone call away. But don't worry about me; you need to fix this with Katie."

"But I-"

"NO! No buts, you are so in love with her it hurts me to see you in pain. I can't picture it in my head because MY best friend is never in pain. So go over to her house, call her, write her a love letter, do something because if you don't then the rest of your life will be nothing but one big what if. So go get your life in order."

"Fine. I'll talk to her after the game tomorrow. Happy?"

"If you will be, then yes."

"You enjoy bossing me around don't you?"

"It puts me to sleep. Speaking of which, I need to. I'll talk to you later, okay?"

"Yeah. Night."

She hung up and I laid my head back and did some thinking.

My life has changed in so many ways. When I got here I was nobody, and now I'm a pretty popular guy. I know it's only because of football, but it's something. When I first came here Katie didn't know I existed. Now I can't picture my life without her.

I just hope it's not too late.

Kiss Me I'm Going to Scream

I woke up today with mixed emotions and a nervous stomach. Just last Friday we won our last playoff game. Today, one week later, was the last game of the year. We were in the state championship. The squad was allowed to go but we had to bring out ponchos. It was supposed to rain bad tonight.

I got up and got dressed. The cheer squad and the football team rode the same bus, and I was hoping to sit anywhere without Luke. He had tried to speak to me after the game last week but I did not want anything to do with him then. The same thing stands tonight.

After giving Dad the directions to the stadium in Columbus, I headed out for the school. Last night we had our pep rally and the whole entire town was going to the game. Every store, diner and gas station was closed and had signs saying 'Good luck Lions!' and 'Feel the Roar!' on them.

The school was even worse. We had painted the entire school, and we held a moment of silence for John. His spirit rock was made a permanent landmark and his number eighteen jersey will be retired next season. Every player and cheerleader, even the fans were wearing support patches on the left of our uniforms.

I walked in the back way of the school and went to the locker room. The rest of the squad was there and we had five minutes to get ready because the bus left in twenty minutes. We were all nervous.

We had never even been that far outside of Eastgate before, now we were going to Columbus. The state capital. This tension was too much.

It was a two hour drive to the stadium, so I had my mp3 to keep me occupied. I left the locker room and bumped into, you guessed it, Luke.

"Oh, sorry." He said.

I didn't answer and walked out the door.

"Is this how it's going to be? You're just going to ignore me forever?"

"Sounds like a pretty good idea to me." I said without looking at him.

"Katie, I'm sorry. Don't be like this."

I turned around sharply. "Like what, Luke? You told me that you wanted to focus on football so congrats, you got your wish."

I turned back around and got on the bus and sat next to the water boy. Luke got on the bus and sat next to the coach. He looked back at me and sighed. I didn't care.

Who am I kidding? Of course I care. I love him. I need him. Without him, I'm completely lost. It was like I was a child and my favorite toy was lost. I needed to fix this but I didn't know how. I guess if I want him, it will be right. Until then I put my earphones back in and waited for the bus to move.

We were on our way.

First Quarter

We sat in the locker room, dead quiet. No one was looking at each other, no one was talking. Everyone was in their own minds. Coach was in the office they gave him and we could tell he was just as nervous as us. I looked up and saw him standing at the door. He surveyed us and cleared his throat.

"Let's go."

We stood up and followed him. We knew our opponents were good. The Yellowjackets were undefeated this year and had one of the best pass defenses in the state. I looked over at the new quarterback, Jake Walters and he was dead chalk white. I patted him on the shoulder pad and put my helmet on, waiting for our introduction.

"And now, from the town of Eastgate, Ohio, with a record of nine wins and four losses. Being led onto the field by Coach Jones, please welcome the Eastgate LIONS!"

We ran out, getting cheered from about half the crowd. I looked all over and was in awe. I never saw a stadium this huge. I went to our sideline and stood, waiting to go out for the coin toss. We walked out and met their teammates. None of them shook our hands, they just glared. So we glared back.

We lost the toss and they chose to receive. So I had to wait it out for a bit. We kicked it off and the ball carrier caught it at our five. He took it all the way to the house. We swore and watched them kick the extra point. We looked up at the scoreboard.

Perrysburg: 7 Eastagte: 0.

I put my helmet on and waited for us to get the ball. We ran it back to our thirty-one, and I ran to the huddle. Jake was shaking and could barely call the play.

"Eighty eight gap, eighty eight gaps."

We broke and I ran to my spot. I was running a post pattern and then a slant. I looked at the safeties lineup and it was shifting. I closed my eyes and waited for the snap.

I felt people moving and bolted. I ran my route and Jake launched the ball my way. As soon as I caught it, I met a safety who laid into me. I held onto the ball and fell to the ground. Something was wrong. I felt my shoulder pop and I couldn't move.

The trainer ran over and took my helmet off. I heard the crowd grow silent and then the doctor's voice.

"Luke, can you hear me?"

I nodded and sat up. They took me to the sideline and took a closer look at my shoulder. It was dislocated. The doctor took a look at Coach.

"He's out for at least three quarters."

I groaned and looked at the floor. I sat there until the end of the first quarter and looked up at the scoreboard.

Perrysburg: 17 Eastgate: 3.

Second Quarter

I saw Luke go down. I gasped and wanted to run to see if he was okay but my better senses told me otherwise. They took him to the sideline and sat him down and I went back to cheering. The game wasn't looking in our favor. We were down by fourteen at the end of the first quarter.

Second quarter we got to take a break. The rain had already started to fall and we had to put our ponchos on. I looked over at Luke, who was upset that he couldn't play. I sighed and went to go to the bathroom. I opened the door and saw someone I didn't expect to see. Nicole was standing there, doing her makeup.

"Nicole?" I asked.

She looked over and had a mixed reaction.

"Hey Katie."

"What are you doing here?"

"I wanted to see the game. I'm only here for tonight though. How's Luke?"

"He's still pretty hurt. They say he won't be ready until the fourth quarter."

"Well . . . he told me about the pregnancy scare."

"Yeah, kind of figured he would."

"Why did you lie? Why lie to him, about that?'

I looked down and sighed.

"He was in pain. I found out that I wasn't pregnant right before his accident and I got scared. I was hurting from his accident and not being a mother at the same time and I panicked."

"Well it's over and done with. Just don't hurt him anymore. He's too good for that."

I nodded and she made her way out.

"Nicole!" I called.

She turned around and looked dead at me.

"About us . . . I'm sorry. I hope that someday we can be friends."

She smiled. "Make things right with Luke and we'll see."

I smiled and watched her leave. I came out of the bathroom and returned just in time to see the final second of the second quarter go off. I looked at the score.

Perrysburg: 31 Eastgate 17.

Halftime

I was helped into the locker room. They sat me in the medical room and examined my shoulder. I saw the coach pacing back and forth and he stopped dead in the middle of the floor and looked at everyone.

"You know, in my fifteen years of coaching, this is my best team. You guys gave it your all this season in the games that you did play. I know not having John here hurts all of you, it hurts me. But right now you are playing like you've already given up. That's not the kind of memory I want this team to have. You men have proven that you are indeed capable of being bigger and better. For John's sake and your own, you owe it to yourselves to be a better person. So go out there and win or lose, give it your all. God knows you can do that."

He went into his office and sat down. We still had a good ten minutes before halftime was over so after the doctor popped my shoulder back into place, I did something I never did before.

"Guys. Look I know most of you don't like me or don't know me. I get that. I get that some of you had to go lower on the list so I could play. Kurt couldn't handle that, and it cost John everything . . . including his own life. John died, and he saved me. So I think we not only owe it to ourselves to become immortal, but we owe it to John. That's not just anybody on your patch. That's your friend, your teammate, and your student. He gave it all for his friends, and his team."

They were all listening and nodding.

"Let's go out there, and make those guys feel the ROAR!"

Everyone was starting to cheer at this point and the feeling we got from it was insanity. We charged out to the field and we knew from then on, no matter what, we were immortal.

Third Quarter

I was cheering as the team ran back out onto the field. We were down by fourteen and we still were without Luke. I looked back at him and he looked at me and we both smiled. This team was excited and we were excited. We knew something special was going to happen.

The rain was pouring down now. The officials wanted to postpone but the fans wouldn't budge. We all wanted to see the end of this game. We got the ball and drove it to their twenty on our first drive. We scored but they responded right back with a score of their own.

I sat down because my ankle was bothering me and watched as both teams went to war with each other. Midway through the third it was still a fourteen point game in Perrysburg's favor. I sighed and told Coach Davis I was taking a break. She nodded and I went to go get something to drink.

As I came back I looked at the scoreboard and saw that we had scored again. I was excited but nervous all the same. I didn't know whether or not we could pull this off. Our tiny town has never really had great football success. It was depressing year after year of letdowns. This town deserves more than that.

I looked up at our section and we were silent. No one was cheering and no one was clapping. This was too much for me to handle. I looked over at my father; he was sitting down and reading a text. I shook my head and grabbed a megaphone.

"Come on guys!" I shouted. A few looked at me.

"I said come on!"

A few people cheered and clapped.

"Listen, your boys need you! Let's hear it for the LIONS!"

The crowd started to cheer a little bit louder.

"Let's go Lions, let's go! Let's go Lions, let's go!"

The crows echoed me until the crowd was louder and screaming their heads off. I smiled and rejoined my squad. We took off our ponchos and riled up the crowd even more. We didn't care if we got soaked. We were having the best time of our lives.

The third quarter ended. I looked over at the score again.

Perrysburg: 34 Eastgate: 31.

fourth Quarter

I was still unable to compete. I paced the sidelines back and forth as I watched my team play. We were midway through the fourth and the score was still thirty-four to thirty-one Perrysburg. I watched as our fans grew louder and louder and my team get better and better. We were all soaked in mud and water on both sides.

I wanted in so bad. I looked over at the clock. A minute thirty left and we were on defense. I was jumping and making noise just as much as everyone else.

It was fourth down for them. They were on our goal line and we were looking at total defeat. They snapped the ball and gave it to their back. He leaped over and I knew we were done. But as I saw him jump, four Lions threw their shoulders into him and he fell back on the three. He didn't get in.

We were cheering and we were insane. But I still wasn't able to compete, so I had to stand out here and watch my team play.

We took over at the three. Jake snapped the ball and threw it to the tight end, who ran it out of bounds at the twenty. Then we threw it to the forty and then ran it to the forty five. We were moving. On the next play we were penalized for offensive pass interference and then we lost a yard. Jake threw an incomplete pass and here we were fourth and sixteen.

I bowed my head before I heard Coach call me.

"Lucas, you're in." I ran off into the field and got in the huddle. Jake was still whiter than white but we calmed him down.

"Eighty eight slant. Eighty eight slant."

We broke. I went to my spot and set myself. I looked at their lineup again. I knew this was going to work. Before Jake snapped, I had the play in mind.

"HIKE!"

I ran into my slant and then in the middle of that broke off into the middle of the field. Jake threw the ball up in the air and as the clock hit zero, I was in the middle of three Yellowjackets. I leaped and before the ball got there, I thought about Katie, about my parents, my dad, John, Nicole, and how much this play didn't matter. As long as I had them I was content. I was happy.

I landed and the crowd was insane. I looked over at our side. We were jumping and cheering. Katie was crying and Coach was smiling. I looked in my hands and there was the football.

We won the state championship.

My teammates met me in the end zone and we all jumped and hugged and cried. This moment would live on in our minds forever. We were immortal, we were champions.

We ran into midfield and met our fans. Everyone was hugging each other and kissing their parents or loved ones. I looked over and saw Nicole and hugged her.

"Oh my God Luke that was amazing! Your dream came true."

She looked over at Katie.

"Now go spend it with the girl who loves you."

I looked over at her, with her tear streaked face and messed up hair. I smiled and walked over to her.

"Hey, nice catch. Very cool."

"Thank you. Nice legs, little long for you."

She hugged me and smiled.

"I guess I'll see you around then, Luke."

She turned to leave and something inside of me took over.

"Katie!" I called.

She turned around and looked at me.

"You forgot something."

She looked confused, and as I walked over to her I knew she could tell what was going to happen.

"You forgot this." I said and my lips met hers. I held her tightly and kissed her time and time again as the rain and the confetti hit us. Nothing would make me let her go, not now not ever. I was in love with her, and she was in love with me. The way I saw it, no state championship could match that.

She broke away from me and looked up into my eyes. I looked back down at her and smiled.

"Luke . . . are we . . . well you know-"

"Dating? As long as you call me your boyfriend."

She smiled and kissed me again. All was right in the world, at least for us.

Perrysburg: 34 Eastagte: 37.

Epilogue

"James! Come on it's your first day you don't want to be late!"

I groaned. My first day of high school already? Dammit. I slowly got up and as I got dressed, I wanted so much to go back to sleep. I walked downstairs yawning and went into the kitchen. I saw my father, Luke and my mom, Katie. They were doing their usual kissing thing they do in the morning.

"Guys come on! Unless you're planning on giving me a sibling, stop."

My mom stood at me open mouthed.

"James Albright Warren!"

I smiled and hugged her.

"Sorry mom, just nerves."

She sighed and messed with my hair.

"Relax, kid. It's only high school."

I laughed and kissed her goodbye. I got in the truck with my dad and we set off.

"So, you excited?" He asked.

"Yeah, a little. Football tryouts are today too."

"Well I think you'll do fine. After all your dad is the coach."

I smiled and looked at the school as we stopped.

"Hey," He said. "What's really bothering you?"

"There's this girl, her name is Jackie. How do I get her to notice me?"

He smiled and looked at me in the face.

"Sometimes kid, love is forbidden. But it's up to you as to whether or not you want that person. So if you like her go and talk to her."

"Is that how you met Mom?"

He nodded and patted me on the shoulder.

I got out and made my way inside Eastgate High School. Something told me I was going to be okay.

After all, I'm a Warren.